THE ITAL

The Dallori brother

Suave and sophisticate...
Antonio and Marco are 100% Italian

DR DALLORI'S BRIDE
Antonio is cool-headed and in control,
but he's definitely hot-blooded.
And single mum Laura Bright is testing his resolve…
Will Antonio be able to use his irresistible
Latin looks to tempt Laura down the aisle…?

DR MARCO'S BRIDE
Marco's determined to be a bachelor;
no woman is going to catch him! But when he catches
the bouquet at Antonio's wedding he starts to wonder
if soon he'll be the one saying 'I do'!

Carol Wood lives with her artist husband on the south coast of England. She has always taken an interest in medical matters, especially general practice and nursing in the community. Her hobbies are walking by the sea, watching wildlife and, of course, reading and writing romantic fiction.

You can find out more about Carol Wood at: www.millsandboon.co.uk

Recent titles by the same author:

DR DALLORI'S BRIDE*
THE IRRESISTIBLE DOCTOR
HER PARTNER'S PASSION
BACK IN HER BED

The Italian Doctors duet

DR MARCO'S
BRIDE

BY
CAROL WOOD

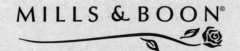

MILLS & BOON

First published in Great Britain 2003
Harlequin Mills & Boon Limited,
Eton House, 18-24 Paradise Road, Richmond, Surrey TW9 1SR

© Carol Wood 2003

ISBN 0 263 83463 8

Set in Times Roman 10½ on 11 pt.
03-0803-54099

Printed and bound in Spain
by Litografía Rosés, S.A., Barcelona

CHAPTER ONE

ONE confirmed pregnancy and an interesting and rather painful case of fasciitis, dropped into the four hours of her very busy Monday morning, had given Dr Kelly Anders plenty of food for thought.

The pregnancy was delightful, a case of IVF treatment that had worked wonders with the spirits of the thirty-something parents who had almost given up hope. And the fasciitis victim, a cricketer, had drawn her into a bear hug when the corticosteriod drugs had begun to kick in and release him from the wincing pain of his foot injury.

Kelly's tall, willowy frame relaxed at the thought of her small but satisfying successes as she bent over her desk, checking the hospital correspondence, her long neck arched in contemplation, one hand curved on the plane of her slender hip.

It was a mini-triumph to have enjoyed four weeks of unadulterated bliss at a new surgery. Patients, staff and her rented waterfront flat were... She lifted her neat chin, set in the centre of her heart-shaped face and closed her thick, dark lashes momentarily over her violet eyes, trying to think of the right word.

Fortuitous...

No way. It was more than that.

Destiny...?

Maybe. A little clichéd to describe the past month as fate. But if it was so, and the forces of her life were coming together in Charbourne Medical Centre, then who was she to dispute it? And if ever she was given a choice to practise medicine, anywhere in the world—

'*Mi scusi...?*'

The softly spoken words brought her out of her thoughts and Kelly turned, her gaze flying to the half-opened door. A dark-haired boy stood there, his beautiful brown eyes blinking slowly under a shock of black hair. His skin reminded her of olives, naturally, luminously tanned, and his full, expressive mouth quirked at the corners, lighting up his face in a smile.

Kelly moved forward, realizing at once that this child had no inhibitions as to whether he should introduce himself. In seconds he was offering her a stream of delicious, if incomprehensible, Italian.

'Speak a little slower.' Kelly chuckled, trying to recall her long-forgotten school Italian and was trying to think of something a little more creative than '*Buongiorno*' when the door swung open again.

A tall, elegantly dressed man entered, his sun-bronzed features and luxuriant ebony hair so similar to the boy's that Kelly had no doubt they were related. A fact that was confirmed in the very next instant as a jet black eyebrow rose instructively over dazzling light blue eyes. 'English, please, Frederico.'

'*Papa…mi spiace, ma—*'

'Frederico…' Again the eyebrow quirked.

The boy blushed under his olive skin, his huge brown eyes melting Kelly's heart even before he spoke. When he did, she was charmed beyond words at his deliciously broken accent.

'My…name is…Frederico.'

'Hello, Frederico.' She smiled again and after a few seconds turned to her second visitor, realizing at once that he was the substitute doctor the practice had long been awaiting. 'Dr Dallori?' she guessed, and he nodded, stretching out cool, firm fingers to tighten over hers with unsurprising power.

Unsurprising, because the expensive grey suit couldn't begin to disguise the powerful, muscular frame beneath the fine fabric. The ruckle across his sleeve denoted tightly packed arm muscle and the black shirt that flashed briefly in the opening of his jacket revealed a broad, hard chest that spoke volumes about his fitness.

'Marco,' he insisted charmingly. 'And you must be Dr Anders.'

'Kelly,' she answered quietly, her eyes lifting to tangle with the most penetrating blue gaze she had ever encountered. 'Welcome to Charbourne. Have you just arrived?'

'Yesterday, but Frederico and I are spending time together today. Tomorrow I shall leave him in the care of his cousin, Isabella, who has accompanied us.'

Kelly smiled down at Frederico again, mentally reviewing what she already knew of Marco Dallori. Jamie Collins had explained that the Italian doctor was thirty-five years of age and for some years a widower, having lost his attractive young wife Sophia to cancer at a tragically young age. Marco was substituting for his brother Antonio, founder member of the practice, until October. *And* he was the man with whom she would be working—heaven help her—for the next few months.

'I am sorry for the intrusion,' he continued in faultless English. 'My son never misses an opportunity to speak, as you have discovered.' He smiled dazzlingly, a set of perfect white teeth flashing between deeply sensual lips. Fortunately for her shocked reactions, Frederico proceeded to forget his father's instruction and relapsed into a roller-coaster of Italian.

'*English*,' Marco Dallori interrupted his son again, raising a tanned and exquisitely manicured hand. 'Our stay in England,' he explained almost apologetically to Kelly, 'has been the cause of much excitement.'

'Naturally.' Kelly shrugged, beaming a conspiratorial smile at Frederico.

'However,' Marco added, casting a glance at his son, 'this holiday will provide an excellent opportunity to improve his English.'

Just then Kelly's phone rang and she answered it, though

her attention was still drawn to the impressive tableau of
father and son. They were so much alike. Remarkable. Just
the eyes differed, one set reminding her of crisp, wet, autumn oak leaves and the other a sky she had seen in the
heart of the Alps of spellbinding turquoise.

'So, shall I send your next one in, Dr Anders?'

'What? Oh, yes, thank you, Michelle.' Kelly dismissed
the snow-capped vision only to find that she was once again
the centre of attention as a pair of deep blue eyes met hers
without faltering.

'We must allow you to continue.'

'I'm sorry.' She smiled, aware that their introduction had
been woefully inadequate but time was pressing and her
list was long. 'It is a little frantic this morning.'

'Then we shall talk later. This evening, if you are free.
I believe we are neighbours.'

Kelly's violet eyes widened as her brain tried to retrieve
the important nugget of information that she must have mis-
laid. '_Neighbours_,' she repeated stupidly, as Frederico
frowned up at them, sensitive to the sudden tension in their
conversation.

'We have an apartment at the marina—as I believe you
do.' Noting her shocked surprise, he added quickly, 'But
you will be relieved to know that we are situated on the
east side, as opposed to the south.' Flashing blue splinters
of amused delight sparkled in his eyes and Kelly realized
he was enjoying the advantage he had over her.

Blushing crimson, Kelly's full mouth twitched as she
attempted to deal with the bombshell he had just landed at
her feet. Not that she had any practical objection. They
wouldn't exactly be living in each other's pockets, yet her
reason for renting the apartment had been that the marina
afforded her complete privacy. A bolt-hole that seemed cus-
tom-made for her needs. The perfect place to spend her
summer, at liberty to live and work as she pleased.

'Let's say seven-thirty? We can relax outside on the terrace if this beautiful June weather holds.' Almost as an

afterthought, he added, 'As neighbours it will be good to get to know one another, no?'

Taking a breath, she nodded politely, mentally scrubbing the evening she had planned. Not that she had made any real friends yet at the marina leisure centre. She could play squash or swim any evening. In effect, this man was acting as her employer. It wouldn't do her any harm to agree. Still, a little shiver slid icily down her backbone.

'This evening, then,' Marco Dallori confirmed. 'Appartment one twenty-two.' His extraordinary blue gaze touched her briefly before he gestured to the boy and together they left her room.

For the rest of the morning Kelly had to fight to keep her concentration. Her ten-minute exposure to Marco Dallori had left her feeling unsettled. With time to reflect, his invitation had bordered closely on a command. She did have a life outside the practice. One that he had assumed she could easily change for his benefit.

However, she consoled herself, his motives might be un-selfish. Introductions in a less official setting would make for a more harmonious relationship. And the man couldn't be held responsible for his looks. He was Italian. The sooner she got used to having him around the better.

Her first patient of the afternoon was eighteen-year-old Tania Farlow who sat anxiously on the edge of her seat. 'I'm starting as a first year at the college of art and design in September,' she explained. 'I'm wondering if I should have the meningitis immunization. My friend had a cold and a stiff neck. It was just flu, but I suppose it worried me a bit.'

'Students can be at risk during their first weeks,' Kelly agreed. 'Do you know the symptoms?'

Tania pushed back her long blonde hair and nodded. 'I read up on them. Aside from headaches and sickness you get a rash, then you do the glass test. You can press a glass against it and see if it fades. If it doesn't change colour then it's bad news.'

Kelly nodded slowly. 'Meningitis and septicaemia are quite rare. But it's better to be safe.'

'Meningitis is a killer, isn't it?'

'Sometimes. But if symptoms are treated quickly people do recover. But, then again, if you're concerned, it's best to go for immunization.'

'Can I have the injection today?'

'We'll have to order it.' Kelly hesitated. 'It'll take about a week.'

'And when I've had it, I'll be safe?'

Kelly nodded. 'Against group A and C meningitis and septicaemia, yes. And you'll only need one dose.' Kelly waited, but it was clear her young patient was doubtful, though about what, Kelly wasn't sure. 'Shall we go ahead and book an appointment?'

'What if…?' Tania stopped, biting her lip. 'I mean, would there be any reason why I shouldn't have it?'

'Only if you think you're ill—or pregnant. But if you're in good health, as you seem to be, I can see no reason why not.'

Eventually Tania nodded. 'All right. I'll have it.'

When the arrangements and further explanations had been made and Tania had gone, Kelly wondered what she had missed. There had been something in Tania's manner that she didn't understand.

'Dr Anders?' Kelly looked up to find Becky Sharpe, the practice nurse, standing in front of her.

'Becky—sorry—I was miles away. Come in.'

'As in Mediterranean miles?' suggested Becky teasingly as she sat down.

'Sorry?' Kelly feigned ignorance, though she could guess what, or rather who, Becky was hinting at.

'Our morning's new arrival…?' Becky prompted.

'Oh, I see,' Kelly sighed, smiling.

'Reception is buzzing. He's a real stunner, isn't he?'

Becky wrinkled her nose. 'Well, all the Dallori men are, actually. Did I tell you that I worked with Laura Bright— Dr Antonio Dallori's new wife?'

Kelly knew she wasn't about to be let off easily. 'No-o...'

'Laura was temporary practice nurse here last year. Dr Antonio delivered her little girl, then offered her a job here while Sam Westward was on maternity leave. Within a few months they'd fallen in love and got married—in Capri.'

Recalling the few non-personal details Jamie Collins had sketched for her at her interview, Kelly nodded slowly. But Becky gave her no time to reply as she rushed on. 'Laura sent us the photos of their wedding. Imagine *Capri*! A dream, really. They're in the cupboard in the staffroom if you're interested.'

'Well, some time maybe.' Kelly smiled, glancing at her watch. 'Is there someone else waiting?'

'Oh, yes. Our Mrs Frost. You haven't met her yet, have you? She's a bit of hypochondriac.'

'All in a day's work,' Kelly mused lightly.

'Actually, Laura was the one who used to deal with her,' Becky said as she rose slowly to her feet. 'She was brilliant with difficult patients, which, I suppose, was all part of her charm.'

'So what does Mrs Frost have today?' Kelly tried again.

'Chest cough and wheezes.'

'OK. Send her in.'

'Don't forget to look at those photos,' Becky reminded her as she walked to the door. 'I mean, that Italian family— they are really something else....'

Becky ground to a halt as a tiny figure appeared beside her. 'Oh, there you are, Mrs Frost.'

The older woman smiled. 'How nice. I'm so relieved we have a lady doctor to take Dr Chandra's place.'

Becky disappeared with a grin and Mrs Frost sat down, explaining her current problem and undoing her blouse as she spoke. 'I expect you'll want to listen to my wheezing.

Nurse Bright always did.' She gave a dainty blink. 'You don't know her by any chance, do you?'

'No, I'm afraid not.' Kelly dutifully placed the stethoscope on her patient's chest.

'She was so kind. Dr Dallori, too.'

'Breathe in, Mrs Frost.'

'They married, you know.'

'And out slowly.'

'Such a handsome nation, the Italians. Have you seen the photos? They were on show for us all to see and—'

'No, Mrs Frost, I haven't. You do have a few crackles so I'm going to prescribe an antibiotic.'

'Thank you, my dear. I'm sure it will do the trick.' The elderly lady rearranged her clothing. 'And thank you for seeing me so swiftly. Nurse Bright was exactly the same, you know. Nothing was too much trouble. They're due back in September, I understand. I wonder if she'll return to work right away or—'

'I've given you a week's course,' Kelly said, steering the conversation in the other direction again. 'Take the pills as prescribed, won't you?'

'Oh, yes, yes.'

Kelly stood up, helping her patient to her feet, and led her slowly along the hall to Reception. 'Can you manage the steps?'

'Oh, yes, thank you, Dr Anders. See you again soon.'

Kelly watched Mrs Frost pause at the desk to talk to Michelle Flowers and Joanne Granger. Their amused glances flicked to Kelly and she grinned, ducking away again to escape to her room.

She had to admit she was curious. Who wouldn't be? At some point she would glance at those photos and draw her own conclusions on the remarkable Dallori family, at least one of whom she was due to meet this evening.

At five-thirty, Kelly tidied her desk and glanced in the mirror above the handbasin. She'd gained a tan over her olive skin that had mellowed to a soft golden glow, the result of her late suppers on the terrace overlooking the marina.

She'd been so lucky to find her small apartment. And even though it was a little more expensive than she'd budgeted for, she hadn't regretted her decision. Not even this morning, when Marco Dallori had informed her he would be living close by.

Blinking her thick, black lashes and drawing a brush through her shining dark hair, she prepared to leave. At least she wouldn't have to spend hours on her hair. She'd had it styled to a soft nape-of-the-neck curve and it was so simple and easy to manage, falling shiningly into place without the hassle of a hair-dryer.

Kelly gazed at her reflection, aware of a sense of calm enveloping her and showing clearly in her huge violet eyes. Sometimes she caught a shadow of the past in their reflection. In rare moments like this her thoughts sometimes drifted back to Tim Baxter and the one real romance of her life, though the memories were still a little guilt-edged at ending it.

Tim was a really sweet human being. If there had been any chemistry between them, it might have worked. But that element had been lacking, though she'd felt comfortable with the tall, fair-haired medical student and had forgone the grand passion.

During one glorious summer when they had worked in Tuscany together she had almost weakened. The atmosphere of sun and sea had been a heady concoction, but it hadn't lasted into the new term. Back at university, in her natural environment, she'd known it was all wrong. It hadn't been fair to Tim to let him think otherwise.

They still sent each other a card at Christmas. Tim was married now, with a baby daughter and a practice. Their friendship had survived, but her mistake had spurred her on to avoid commitment. And it had worked. She'd had no nightmares lately. No waking in damp sheets, as frightened

as the insecure child she had once been. She'd left the past
behind and had found strength and peace in her career.

Kelly said goodnight to the receptionists and walked
through the wide glass doors into the soft evening air. The
sycamore trees circling the car park were a sea of shimmering green and the purr of seaside traffic was a soothing
contrast to the pounding of the city.

Moving from the Midlands had been the best thing she
had ever done. It had seemed right from day one. The other
doctors, Jamie Collins, Liam Ray and Di Saunders, were
all so helpful. She had felt welcome right from the start.

Kelly paused before unlocking her car and turned to
study the building she had just left. A milky pink sky
stretched over its smooth, blue-tiled roof. She trapped her
lip and gazed thoughtfully from her deep violet eyes. She
was still unable to believe she was part and parcel of this
practice. But as the clock in the slim white tower struck
six, she gave a little start.

Better not get smug just yet, she advised herself quickly.

She still had this evening to get through.

A thought suddenly struck her. Was Marco acting for his
brother, Antonio, discreetly assessing her suitability? The
senior partner might not have been entirely satisfied with
Jamie Collins's assessment—but he *would* trust his
brother's judgment.

Was she on trial? The thought struck her as logical. It
provided the answer for the Italian's doctor's attitude today.
A heaviness formed in her stomach. Her confidence had
been premature. There was no doubt she felt right for
Charbourne Medical Centre. But could she prove she was
the right doctor for the practice?

A question that Marco Dallori would no doubt be asking
himself this evening—and over the foreseeable future.

It was a shimmering evening with a hazy sun dancing on
the water and Kelly decided she would treat the occasion

as informally as possible. After a shower and a liberal coating of moisturizer, she scrambled into fresh clothes.

Her light linen suit had taken the brunt of the day's onslaught and it was a relief to change into fresh white trousers and a lavender tie-waist shirt. Her light summer clogs were comfortable as opposed to the fashionable heels she had been wearing all day, and a dab of scent behind each ear lobe was her only concession to extravagance.

One glance in her bedroom mirror was enough to tell her that she had selected her clothes wisely. Her dark hair fell naturally to the nape of her neck, haloing her heart-shaped face, and the light dusting of make-up on eyes and lips was all she needed to complete her outward confidence.

As for the inner turmoil that had suddenly manifested itself, she was attempting to quell it. Her busy day hadn't managed to distance her enough from the memory of those unsettling light blue eyes that had searched her so intently. Or the manner in which he had so efficiently brought about this meeting. Perhaps it had something to do with the boy who, unlike his father, had gained her trust immediately.

Collecting her bag from the lounge, she noticed the room radiated a golden glow from the evening sun that streamed in. Though her one-bedroomed apartment was not over-large, the marina was visible from almost all the rooms. She loved the changing scenes and watching the boats tethered to their brightly coloured buoys. Sailing craft, speedboats, catamarans and cruisers bobbed side by side. Their owners either busied themselves on the decks or sat with friends on the pontoons or by the jetties, enjoying the tangerine sun that slid toward the horizon.

Kelly waved to several boat owners as she set off. She had come to know the faces of the boating community and, having sailed herself since childhood, she was no stranger to the sea.

The complex was an imposing E-shape, and each dwelling had its own private access to the marina. But she had never strolled the length of the path to the east side.

Choosing to walk rather than drive this evening, Kelly took the brief fifteen minutes to consider why it was that she felt so apprehensive.

Marco Dallori had been nothing more than polite and it would be ridiculous to assume that pressure was being brought upon her this evening. But by the time she reached apartment one hundred and twenty-two, she had only re-inforced her early conclusions.

His low-rise apartment lay at the end of a terrace, stra-tegically positioned for views of the marina at its rear. The area at the front was filled with a wide velvet green lawn and shrubs that spilled over the pebbled walkway to the front door. An aroma of a barbecue was in the air, curling deliciously around the rooftops, and voices were coming from the back, one of which she thought she recognized.

But even before she pressed the bell, the door opened and she was enveloped in a pair of piercing blue eyes that immediately shattered her practiced composure. They were neither light nor dark, but somewhere in between, the un-nerving quality making her suddenly aware of their intense sexual allure.

A fact that she could have well done without acknowl-edging at just this moment as she stood nervously on the doorstep.

'Kelly, please, come in.' Marco's voice was dark and even and had a slight rumble to it which made the total effect of his presence electrifying. As she stepped in, he looked even taller than this morning, wearing a light-coloured shirt and trousers that looked expensively under-stated.

Perhaps the depth of his tan and the darkness of his hair made an even more stunning contrast to the soft cuttlebone colours that radiated from the interior of the apartment. But the overall effect had her taking a breath and forcing a rather bewildered smile to her lips. 'I'm a little early...'

'Not at all. I was waiting for you.'

Kelly tried not to read too much into that. He had important questions in mind—obviously. Was this to be an entirely formal discussion?

He closed the door and Kelly gazed around her, clearing her throat. 'I really hadn't realized these were such large apartments,' she said politely, hoping to set a neutral tone for whatever it was that lay ahead.

'I flew over very briefly two months ago in order to select a property that would be appropriate to our needs. There is a separate annexe for Isabella, and Frederico has a study and bedroom with an *en suite* bathroom. I viewed many places, but this was by far the best.'

Kelly stood in awe, for the apartment was luxurious and there was no doubt that Marco had taken pains in his selection, which led her to think that the man standing beside her was something of a perfectionist.

'Isabella and Frederico,' he told her, gesturing the room on his right, 'are outside at the moment, but they will join us later.'

Kelly walked into a room that was pure luxury. The polished floorboards shone in the evening sunshine and the rugs that lay across them drew on elements of the ocean, all in an ultra-modern design.

Unframed seascape pastels hung on the pale walls and light wood furniture adorned spaces where the natural light from the wide uncurtained windows showed it at its best. The room led naturally through wide glass patio doors onto the terrace. Beyond this, Kelly could see Frederico and a dark-haired girl splashing in the translucent blue water of a rectangular swimming pool.

'Their energy is inexhaustible.' Marco grinned as he gestured to the sofa. 'Please, make yourself comfortable.'

'Isabella is Frederico's cousin, you said?' Kelly sank onto the sofa and into the pearly white cushions that clustered at her back.

'She is my elder bother's daughter. When Antonio suggested I should come to England, Pietro and his wife asked me if I would bring Isabella. She is eighteen and studying to be a translator. This holiday will be an excellent learning opportunity for her as well as for Frederico. And while I am at work, Frederico will be in the best of care.'

'You have a large family?' Kelly asked uncertainly, recalling Becky's words earlier that day.

He chuckled as he made himself comfortable in a large tub chair opposite her, shifting his large, loose-limbed body until it rested easily. 'There are five of us. Antonio is the youngest, I am next, then Luca, Pietro and Roberto.'

She nodded slowly, the almost musical Italian names flowing stirringly in her thoughts. He smiled, his mouth curving upward in that charming and, she suspected, deliberately focused way. He added lightly, 'I think a girl in the family would have been very welcome for my mother, especially after my father died. Sadly, it was not meant to be.' He paused, crooking an eyebrow. 'Though Antonio as a boy showed little interest in medicine, our father's chosen profession. He loved to be in the kitchen with Mamma.'

Kelly laughed softly. 'But don't most Italians have a gift for food?'

'That is true,' he agreed with a faint smile. 'Good food and wine are part of our culture.' He paused, frowning slightly as he searched her face. 'And you, Kelly? What do you like? Tell me something about yourself.'

'I enjoy good food, too.' She shrugged, knowing that her reply was not a real answer to his question but feeling it was adequate in the circumstances. 'And I do have a soft spot for pasta....'

'Ah...you do?' His black eyebrows rose, unconcerned by her attempt to dodge his enquiry. 'Then we already have a lot in common.'

Kelly stared at him in surprise, aware of the raw physical impact of this man who she hardly knew but who in some way had already begun to get under her skin. His eyes centred on her with the kind of intensity that made it impossible for her to look away.

'Perhaps we should investigate the local restaurants together,' he continued, sitting forward. 'Antonio has given me several excellent recommendations. My suggestion may seem a little presumptuous. But I take no pleasure in eating out alone and as we are both new to Charbourne and share a love of good food…?' He left his sentence unfinished, raising a questioning eyebrow.

Kelly felt her composure fly out of the window. Had he just asked her out? This definitely wasn't what she had expected.

'The idea does not appeal to you?' he asked at once.

'It's not that,' she flustered, 'but we have only—'

'Just met?' he finished for her, his magnetic gaze searching her face as a disquieting trace of amusement flowed briefly through the deep turquoise pools.

'I…I suppose I do mean that,' she admitted, unable to prevent the colour rushing to her cheeks.

'Kelly, you are a very intelligent young woman who shares my interest in medicine—which is obviously our focus in life. While I am in England, I would very much enjoy the company of someone on the same wavelength. The arrangement will not affect our work but, I hope, be a pleasant distraction for us both. If you feel that it will not be right for you, then I will understand and will say no more on the subject.'

She fought to get a grip on herself and managed to keep a composed smile in place. 'You're very direct.'

'Yes.' He nodded. 'It has been said that I am.'

'Marco…' She hesitated. 'I'm not sure if, in the circumstances, it would be a very good idea.'

'Why not?'

'Well,' she flustered a little shakily, 'for one thing, we'll be working together every day. Don't you think that socializing as well might be, well, tempting fate?'

'Not at all,' he said reasonably, as though it had been the most natural thing in the world to make such a suggestion. 'I trust that a few simple excursions would not jeopardize our working relationship. Either one of us would soon call a halt, I am certain, if the pleasure became a burden.'

Kelly didn't know whether she was more shocked at the confidence with which he had asked her out or the indecision that she felt about refusing him. She should refuse, of course. It was far too much of a risk. She was to work with the man, for heaven's sake.

What if they had nothing in common—or even disliked each other? But Kelly knew deep down that it was not dislike she feared, or incompatibility. It was something far more disturbing, which even now she sensed rather than acknowledged consciously.

'I can see I have shocked you,' he said, lifting his mouth in a deliciously sexy smile that had Kelly fighting the overwhelming urge to swallow hard.

'This evening isn't quite going as I had expected,' she admitted ruefully.

He nodded slowly, a smile turning the corners of his wide, full mouth. 'I hope it is proving…better than you had anticipated.'

Kelly couldn't resist a smile. He was certainly a man of few words. Her little chuckle turned into a soft curl of laughter. She had never met a man like Marco Dallori before. 'I'm sorry,' she apologised, clearing her throat. 'I didn't mean to laugh.'

'I like your laughter,' he assured her calmly, his voice melting every bone in her body as his eyes locked with hers. 'It's a beautiful, melodious sound.'

Kelly's violet eyes darkened. 'You have a way with words,' she murmured, hanging on to her composure by a thread. A very thin thread.

The black eyebrow danced teasingly. 'Dare I hope your answer to my question is a yes?'

She paused for a moment, heart pounding, pulse soaring. She was plainly at risk of endangering her goal of an uncluttered summer. She had planned the next six months as the perfect opportunity to assess the potential for her future without any emotional distractions that might influence her, one way or the other.

Yet here she was, staring into the eyes of probably the most provocative and unsettling man she had met in her life, her emotions as distant from being serene and tranquil as they could possibly be.

'We'll see,' she heard herself replying unimaginatively, feeling horribly disappointed in herself as a result.

But not so Marco, whose fine classical features remained unchanged under his thick black cap of hair, his eyes refusing to move from her own. He merely smiled and held her gaze as though words were superfluous to his need.

It was only when the wide glass doors leading to the garden slid open and two wet figures came running in that he finally set her free, turning his attention to his son and niece, allowing Kelly to draw a silent sigh of relief.

CHAPTER TWO

WITH a sense of disbelief, Kelly found herself in the midst of the Dallori family, answering Isabella's questions about her life and her student days, which held such interest for the young woman whose purpose was one day to work in England. Dark-eyed and raven-haired, Isabella was no exception to the Latin looks of the family, and Frederico and the girl, she thought, could easily have been brother and sister.

It was Marco's suggestion that they adjourn to the poolside and relax in the big, luxurious steamer chairs. Isabella and Frederico, having changed into jeans and T-shirts, talked exuberantly to Kelly, Isabella's English proving to be almost as faultless as her uncle's, whilst Frederico had them all amused at his charming broken English. Marco, meanwhile, listened quietly, his elegant, agile body at ease on the long padded chair, his head inclined attentively, as dusk settled around them and a soft breeze rippled the surface of the blue pool water.

His penetrating gaze rarely left her, and as Kelly tried to reorganize her thoughts whilst Isabella spoke, she was sensitive to the heat of his gaze as it flowed over her skin.

After finishing her delicious drink, topped by fresh fruit and a little stick umbrella, Kelly said she must leave, much to the disappointment of Isabella and Frederico.

'Dr Anders has endured quite enough of our company for one evening,' Marco interrupted their protests, rising to his feet. Against the rose pink and blue sunset he looked tall and disconcertingly handsome and Kelly forced herself to move her long, slender legs, which had suddenly become like cotton wool as she slid off the lounger.

'It's been a lovely evening.' She thanked them as Marco led the way over the terrace and Frederico and Isabella walked on either side of her.

'I'll walk you back to your apartment,' Marco insisted as they arrived at the front door, but Kelly quickly shook her head.

'Please, don't trouble yourself,' she insisted, aware of the young people gazing curiously at them. 'It's a beautiful evening. I'll enjoy the stroll.'

For one moment his eyes narrowed slightly at the firm rejection, but then he nodded. 'As you wish.'

'Thank you again.' She smiled politely.

'Goodnight, Kelly.'

'Goodnight,' she returned, deliberately avoiding eye contact. 'Isabella, Frederico.'

'*Arrivederci*,' they both said at once, Frederico giggling and Isabella wreathed in smiles.

She turned at the end of the pebbled path as Frederico called out. It was Italian and she didn't understand it, but she waved, catching one last glimpse of her hosts.

When she was halfway home and the beating of her heart had subsided, she breathed in deeply. For the past two hours she had existed on shallow breathing and it was intoxicating to gulp in the fresh ocean air.

She was in no hurry to arrive home. The breeze seemed like the brush of butterfly wings against her cheeks. The tinkle of spinnakers was a lullaby, soothing her scattered senses. She didn't want the night to end. Tomorrow would come too soon. Tomorrow—and facing Marco Dallori, in reality.

Thoughts of a similar nature were also filling Marco's unusually preoccupied mind as he watched the graceful, slender figure of the young woman disappear into the balmy evening. Something about those deep and lustrous violet eyes was at odds with the firm yet polite rebuff that she had just given him.

Had he been wrong when he had sensed a strong sexual attraction between them when they had first met? It was with an unsettling but single-minded honesty that he answered the question that had demanded an answer ever since he had laid eyes on his beautiful new English colleague.

For the very first time since Sophia had died, he had met a woman he wanted to know more about. Not just more—he wanted to know *everything* about her. And with a satisfied smile that flickered over his full and sensual lips, he made up his mind to do just that. He would indeed discover more about this young woman—by whatever means were available to him. Despite her attempts to keep him at arm's length, he had no intention of allowing her to succeed. Not this time. Not when gut instinct assured him she was so very, *very* different...

The following morning Kelly arrived at work, wondering if she could be honest enough to admit that she had risen an hour earlier and paid special attention to her appearance, shampooing, conditioning and blow-drying her deep brown hair into a soft, bouncy curve around her face and adding her make-up carefully.

The suit of soft ivory linen, which she had bought for her interview, hadn't had any use in the month she had been here. It was a perfect fit, its lines cut closely to her tall, willowy figure, and the soft material looked every inch the designer fabric that it was.

She'd not skimped on her appearance when she'd come to meet Jamie Collins and had been grateful for the cool style and touch of chic. But the confidence it had given her had been worth the small fortune it had cost and she felt that today, of all days, she needed the same type of confidence again.

She met Jamie Collins as she walked through Reception and they headed down the hallway to their rooms. His small but energetic form and his curly light brown hair made him look every inch the ideal family doctor, and he didn't disappoint his patients. Kelly had liked him from the word go. She had met his wife and two children and had come to the conclusion Antonio Dallori's choice of junior partner was faultless.

'You met Marco yesterday?' Jamie asked, shuffling an assortment of papers under his arm and juggling his case at the same time. 'Sorry I didn't have time to make introductions. I was out on an emergency.'

'No worries.' Kelly smiled. 'He called in briefly....'

'And...?' Jamie's wry grin made her laugh.

'And he seems a very nice man.'

Jamie's small, round face crumpled into a smile. 'Oh, good. Great, in fact. I wonder if you'd do me a favour in that case. Go with him on a few calls this week—you know, show him around a bit.'

Kelly was about to protest that she was still finding her way around Charbourne herself when Jamie's mobile shrieked.

'OK, I'll be over,' he groaned under his breath, raising his eyebrows as he slipped the mobile back in his pocket. 'The police—we're on call for them this week. Some nutter going bananas in the cells. I'll have to fit it in now before I start in case he wreaks havoc.' He beamed her a smile. 'So I'll leave Marco with you, Kelly, OK?'

Without giving her time to reply, he flew back along the hall to Reception and Kelly continued to her room. She glanced quickly at the correspondence Maggie Stevens, the secretary, had left on her desk, then wondered if she dare look in on Marco before she started. She didn't know if she was quite ready to face him again after last night. But she didn't have to consider the problem for long as Marco tapped on the door and entered.

He came towards her, his tall, lean body as stunningly attired as before, in a lightweight dark jacket that dropped smoothly from his broad shoulders, combining a stone-washed shirt beneath that would have looked unremarkable on a less powerful physique. His black hair grew down to his collar, thick and glossy, and she found herself locked into that dazzling blue gaze which had lost none of its intensity overnight.

'You look enchanting this morning, Kelly,' he told her easily, causing her to wonder why she was so unprepared for flattery. After last night, she shouldn't be surprised at anything he said. But she was shocked yet again, her cheeks warming as he stood before her, looking more like a mythical figure of ancient Rome clad in modern-day clothing.

The gleam in those blue eyes now seemed splintered with the most beautiful silver in the morning light and his deeply tanned skin radiated health and vitality.

'Thank you,' she said, and managed a smile, but somehow kept it professional enough despite her blush. She had to keep focused and not allow herself the luxury of believing that Marco Dallori was any more interested in her than any other—as he put it—intelligent woman on his wavelength.

Anyway, last night's little episode might just have been a very smooth introduction for purposes that she had not yet discounted. It still wasn't beyond belief that Antonio wanted a personal appraisal from someone he could trust. But if that was so, and Marco chose to go about it in a rather unconventional way, it shouldn't matter to her. And it didn't.

Her priority was her job—discovering if she was happy enough here to accept a partnership—and if Marco Dallori had his own agenda, well, so be it.

'I thought I should speak to you before the day begins,' he said in a deep, husky voice that had her heart beating heavily and making a mockery of her so-called composure. 'You may not have understood Frederico last night.'

'As I left, you mean?' she asked hesitantly.

'He asked if you would call again. I hope you will forgive me if I told him that I hoped it would be soon.'

Kelly stared at him, trying to read the razor-sharp mind

that always seemed two jumps ahead of her. She sensed the deep, drugging sensation of his subtle authority, but she had no intention of being railroaded into a decision she wasn't yet ready to make.

'I think we should be discussing our patients,' she said coolly, avoiding an answer. 'After all, that's what we're here for.'

A smile touched his full mouth. 'Your efficiency and enthusiasm, Kelly, is remarkable.'

He was incorrigible! Kelly shook her head, unable to repress a smile. 'Are you deliberately trying to shatter my concentration first thing in the morning?'

His deep laughter was infectious. 'If I have, then I promise to repair it—as soon as you will allow.'

Kelly knew that she was rapidly losing the battle of words, though she had the distinct feeling it would probably be one of many and she had no intention of losing them all. 'Thank you, Marco, but I have a full list this morning, as I'm sure you do.'

'Indeed—enough to begin with.' He walked to the door and paused, turning back with a familiar little gleam in his eye. 'But should I need enlightenment on any issue…?'

'Liam Ray is in the room at the end of the hall, as I'm sure the girls have already explained,' she said sweetly, then felt guilty as she saw the look of disappointment on his face. 'But if there's anything I can help with…'

He waved his hand lightly. 'Don't worry, Kelly. I am only teasing. Oh, but there is one thing more…'

'Why am I not surprised?' she sighed softly, one eyebrow twitching.

His face was a picture of innocence. 'Jamie has advised we make calls together.…'

'Ye-es…' She nodded slowly. 'He did mention it.'

'Shall we do this today?'

She tried to hide her smile. 'I think not, Marco. You'll have more than enough on your first day to contend with.'

He conceded a nod. 'In that case, I'll look forward to

working with you in the near future, Kelly.' He flashed he
one last slow grin, which did unmentionable things to he
already distracted senses, then slowly closed the door be
hind him.

Kelly sat quietly for a while, trying to haul her thought
together. Was this man for real? She had no way of know
ing. What she did know was that he'd amused her, flattered
her—and made her uncomfortably aware that she was as
vulnerable to Latin charm and persuasion as the nex
woman.

But he had also reminded her of the delicacy of her po
sition. He probably hadn't intended to, but she was a tem
porary member of staff and even a mild flirtation with a
co-worker, let alone her employer's brother, would be an
act of mindless stupidity.

It had taken her a long time to get back on an even kee
after Tim, and the last two years hadn't been easy as she'c
tried to establish her career. Did she really need to jeop
ardize her future just when she was on the brink of making
a major decision in her life?

The answer, of course, was no.

Kelly gave a little sigh, consigning Marco and the un
deniable fact that he was hugely attractive to the back o
her mind, and rang through to Reception for her first pa
tient.

For the rest of the week, Kelly alternated between her sur
geries and her calls, the majority of them to patients she
had treated during her short time at Charbourne. Marco
accompanied her on some of these when time allowed. She
either drove him in her car or he drove her in a large dark
green saloon which he had leased for the duration of his
stay.

Marco was charming and humorous with the patients
who were all, of course, delighted to meet him. Jamie's
idea of driving him to and from calls had worked, she re
alized, because by Friday Marco had memorized most of

the catchment area and could recall with ease the houses and patients they had visited.

But it was at five-thirty on Friday evening, as they returned to the surgery, that Kelly's mobile rang and Kelly stopped the car to answer the call from Reception.

'A Mr James just phoned,' Joanne explained hurriedly. 'His wife, Hannah, is in labour, but it's not going too well. She's Liam's patient, but he's out on an emergency. Any chance you're free?'

'What's the situation, Jo?'

'Her contractions have started and stopped again. She's almost full term. The poor man seemed very distressed.'

'OK, where do they live?'

'Six, Foxglove Close, close to the town centre.'

'No problem, we're almost there,' Kelly replied, flipping off the mobile and glancing at Marco who was listening attentively.

She repeated what Joanne had told her as she drove on towards the white clock tower that marked the circular route around town, and within a few minutes they entered the narrow lane bordered by terraced cottages.

Phillip James answered the door of number six. He was a slim man with light brown hair and an anxious expression that made him look far older than his mid-thirties. He led them up a flight of stairs to a double bedroom where his heavily pregnant wife, Hannah, lay fully dressed on the bed.

'Tell me what's been happening, Mrs James,' Kelly said as she sat down and Marco stood with Phillip James.

The woman, also in her mid-thirties, pushed back her damp blonde hair and eased herself up on one elbow. 'I started contractions yesterday and Phil called the midwife. She examined me but told us to wait until they were every five minutes before ringing the hospital. But that just hasn't happened.'

'So the last one was when?' Kelly asked with a frown.

'About ten...fifteen, minutes ago.'

Kelly nodded. 'OK, well, let's check to see how you're doing.' But as she spoke, she heard a groan behind her and turned to see Phillip slumping against the wall. Marco leapt forward to catch him and, supporting his weight with powerful arms, he carefully lowered him into a chair.

'He hasn't slept or eaten,' Hannah cried out as Kelly gently restrained her from jumping off the bed.

'It's all right,' Marco said as he hunkered down beside her husband. 'He's coming round now.'

'I...I don't know what happened then.' Phillip held his head in his hands. 'Everything went black.'

'Do you have another bedroom?' Marco asked him. 'I think you should lie down for a few minutes.'

'Yes, there's one next door,' Hannah answered for him. 'Please, do as the doctor asks, Phil.'

After a few moments, when her husband had recovered sufficiently to stand up, Marco helped him out of the room, though Kelly could see he was reluctant to leave and it was only at Marco's insistence that he complied.

After rinsing her hands, Kelly helped Hannah with her clothing and as the next contraction took place she was able to determine that Hannah was not yet ready to give birth.

'Your cervix hasn't dilated sufficiently,' she explained gently as she helped Hannah rearrange her clothing. 'We want you to be about ten centimetres, then you'll be well on your way.'

'I'm so worried about Phil,' Hannah confessed, holding back her tears. 'He's determined to be with me when I have the baby. We've done all the parentcraft classes together and he's taken time off work to be with me this week. We want this baby so much.'

Just then there was a tap on the door and Marco entered. 'Your husband will be fine,' he assured Hannah as he took a seat beside the bed.

'Really?'

Marco nodded. 'And how are you?'

'Couldn't run a marathon.' She laughed as tears filled her eyes.

'Your husband is hoping to be with you at the birth?'

Hannah gave a little sniff. 'He wants it more than anything. He was married before, you see.' She bit her lip hard. 'His wife had an ectopic pregnancy when they were abroad and it wasn't diagnosed until it was too late. They couldn't save her…'

'I'm sorry,' Marco said softly, his glance briefly meeting Kelly's. 'It is only to be expected, then, that he is anxious.'

Hannah nodded, laying her head back on the pillows and closing her eyes as Marco stood and gestured to Kelly.

'You're going to admit her?' he asked quietly as they stood in the hall, and Kelly nodded.

'Her contractions aren't strong enough. She'll need pain relief and maybe they'll want to induce her. But with what they've been through, it's going to be an uphill struggle.'

'In that case, the most efficient course,' he murmured, frowning slightly, 'would be for you to drive her to the hospital. Calling an ambulance will only increase her stress levels. And you'll have her there in just a few minutes without any fuss.'

'That's a good idea.' Kelly nodded. 'But what about her husband?'

'Leave him to me.' Marco grinned. 'I shall feed him and have him at the hospital in time to witness the birth of his child.'

Kelly smiled ruefully. 'Would you lay a bet on that?'

He raised a casual eyebrow. 'Why not?'

Ten minutes later, Kelly drove Hannah to the hospital, whilst Marco remained behind to whip eggs and milk and a sprinkling of cheese in the James's tiny cottage kitchen.

A while later they were on their way back to the surgery. A healthy seven-pound-four-ounce baby boy had been born and, as Marco had predicted, Phillip had participated fully in the birth of his son, cutting the cord with tears of relief and joy spilling down his cheeks.

Marco sat quietly as Kelly drove, his loose-limbed body at ease, his long, muscular legs stretched out, his suit jacket folded across them. Out of the corner of her eye Kelly caught the glitter of gold on his wrist—a heavy, masculine watch that caught the glare of street lighting. Black whorls of dark hair clustered on his bronzed skin and spiralled upward to the turned cuffs of his white shirt which looked so amazingly fresh after their long day.

'You're very quiet,' she murmured as the lights of the town twinkled around them.

'I'm feeling privileged.' He smiled as his eyes met hers as she turned briefly to gaze into them. 'Privileged to have been part of today.'

'Me, too.' She nodded. 'I would have lost my bet, wouldn't I?'

He laughed. 'I'm afraid so.'

'I don't know how you managed it, but he seemed a different man when you got him to the hospital.'

'Maybe it had something to do with the way I drove his car.' He chuckled, turning a little and snaking an arm along the back of her seat.

'You drove?'

He nodded. 'I didn't want us to get wrapped around a tree. He was eager to follow after he'd eaten—a little too eager. After explaining that I am fully insured, he handed over the keys. It was an automatic and I hadn't driven one of those in years. I must say, I enjoyed the experience.' His mouth quirked into a rueful smile. 'But I am not so certain about Mr James. At least it took his mind off other matters.'

Kelly laughed, realizing how easy their relationship had become. She felt inexplicably at peace with the world. Who was this man sitting beside her who she knew so little of? Had he been thinking of Sophia when Hannah had told them about the death of Phillip's first wife? What kind of woman had Sophia Dallori been? Had she been as beautiful as her melodious Italian name?

Suddenly Kelly wanted to know all about Marco. More than that. *Needed* to know. It was like a thirst that she couldn't slake, leaving her foolishly desiring an intimacy she knew she couldn't have.

'Will Frederico still be up?' she asked quickly, recalling Marco had phoned home from the hospital.

'I think not. They had swum in the pool all day and Isabella sent him to shower. At home, he is in bed by nine o'clock. My housekeeper makes certain the rules are kept if I am not there.'

Kelly felt a twinge of guilt. He showed no self-pity, but it couldn't be easy to lose a wife and raise a son and still hold down a career. Yet he seemed to have done all these things effortlessly, though, of course, she didn't know what lay behind the handsome, sensual features that always looked so calm and composed.

'Kelly, are you on call this weekend?' he asked, breaking into her thoughts.

'Yes, I am,' she answered hesitantly. 'Why?'

'I wondered if you would join us for dinner.'

Kelly kept her eyes on the road. Thank heaven she was on call. To have refused him point blank might have been impossible. 'I'm sorry.' She shrugged.

'Another time perhaps.'

She didn't reply as her heart skittered wildly under her ribs and suddenly a deep tension filled the air. What was happening to her? Why was she unable to separate her confused feelings about Marco Dallori?

The practice was in darkness when they reached it and she switched off the lights and engine, intending to climb out of the car and allow him to go to his. But her heart nearly stopped as he reached out and held her wrist.

'Are you annoyed with me?' he asked, and she sank back against her seat.

'No. I'm not annoyed.'

'But?'

'But…nothing. I appreciate all you did today. And we worked together well.'

He turned shining pools of blue silver on her, which glimmered like precious jewels in the reflection of the street lighting. 'Yes, we did. Which is why I would like to be with you, Kelly…to talk to you…to understand more about you.'

She felt the colour flood to her cheeks. The thought of seeing him was not only exciting, but what, deep in her heart, she really wanted. Yet knew it would be the height of foolishness if she were to agree.

'I don't think so, Marco.'

'Then we seem to have come full circle,' he sighed wearily. 'And I had hoped we had advanced from our first meeting.'

She sat quite still, her heart pounding so loudly in her chest she thought he must be able to hear it. The car felt claustrophobic and his searching gaze was too intense, too demanding to escape. 'We have advanced,' she agreed tightly. 'And it's because we work well together that I don't want to compromise our relationship. I think you know what I mean.'

She was a liar, but she prayed he didn't suspect it. More than anything she wanted to know him, really know him, but she was afraid of the feelings that he had brought to life inside her. She never did anything by halves. She had to put her whole heart and soul into everything. Her senses told her it would be no different with the man whose light touch had just fallen from her wrist and left it feeling as though it was burning.

She didn't trust herself to accept one invitation and turn down another. She would want more, craving something she just couldn't have. He was from another culture, another world, with responsibilities and commitments that had no place in her life, just as she had no place in his.

'It's late,' she said quickly, shocked and angry with her-

elf as she let herself out of the car and stepped into the
warm night. It seemed an eternity before he came to stand
beside her, the scent of his aftershave filling the air, fuelled
with the body heat that swept intoxicatingly from his body.

'If that is what you wish, Kelly, we shan't speak of such
things again,' he said, and cleared his throat.

It's not what I wish, but what I have to do, she cried out
silently, knowing that if she voiced her feelings he would
only argue with her, as he had before, and she would lose,
going back on the vow that she had made to herself.

More than anything, she wanted to see him again. Of
course she did. She couldn't help herself. She was more
attracted to him than to any man she had ever known. But
even she could see there was no future in getting to know
a man who was staying just a few short months in the
country.

She had carved out a career. Her full attention was focused on her work—that was what she'd promised herself.
It would be reckless and juvenile to lose sight of her goals.

But as he bent and brushed a kiss on her cheeks, whispering tenderly, '*Buonanotte,* Kelly,' she felt just that—
reckless and juvenile.

And it was all she could do to keep her hands from
sliding around his neck and drawing him to her and forgetting who—and what—she was.

CHAPTER THREE

As THE days passed, Kelly found her patient base increasing, keeping her busy until well after routine hours. Jamie Collins and Liam Ray split the temporary residents between them and Marco took care of the emergency visits.

He made no attempt to single her out, which made her feel perversely disappointed. He was always charming, as he was to all the staff and patients. And he'd been so swift to find his way around that their making calls together had become unnecessary after that first week.

As a hot July unfolded, Kelly decided to call on Tania Farlow. It was almost a week since her missed appointment, despite several attempts to reach her. Kelly found the house quite easily, an old Victorian building divided into flats and bedsits. She pressed the communal bell and eventually a young woman answered, dressed in a long T-shirt, baggy track pants and flip-flops.

'Does Tania Farlow lives here?' Kelly asked as the girl yawned, appearing to have just climbed out of bed.

'Yes, we share a flat. Who are you?'

'I'm her GP and it is rather important that I speak to her.'

'Oh.' The girl bit her lip. 'To be honest, Tania's not very well.'

'I'm sorry to hear that. Perhaps I can help.'

'I don't know if she'd want to see you.' She looked quickly back at the stairs, then shrugged. 'She had a bit of a row with her boyfriend a couple of hours ago and she's in quite a state.'

Kelly wondered what she meant by 'state'. 'Could you

ask her all the same? As I said, it's quite urgent that I speak to her.'

After a pause, the girl opened the door. 'OK, but you'll have to wait here, in the hall.'

Kelly stepped in, recognizing the familiar sights, smells and sounds of her own student days. Bicycles leaning against the grubby walls, the smell of burnt toast and someone's music playing loudly at the top of the house as a jumble of bags, shoes, instrument cases and a surf board lurked untidily under the stairs.

Five minutes later no one had appeared and Kelly was wondering what to do next when she saw Tania standing at the top of the uncarpeted stairs.

'Oh, it's you, Dr Anders,' she said, not moving down them.

'Hi, Tania.' Kelly walked forward, startled at her appearance. She looked thinner, paler and her long silky blonde hair hung limply around her shoulders. To Kelly's dismay she saw that the right-hand side of her face was deeply bruised, a large, unsightly patch of purple skin having swollen around her eye.

'What did you want?' Tania asked quickly.

Kelly shrugged. 'You missed your appointment.'

'Oh, I…I forgot, sorry. I had a bit of an accident.' Tania looked uncomfortable as she stood there. 'I fell off my boyfriend's motorbike.'

'Were you hurt?'

'No. I'm fine now.'

'Are you sure?' Kelly moved towards the stairs, but Tania stepped back nervously.

'No…no…really, I'm fine.'

'If you're in trouble, maybe I can help.'

'There's nothing you can do. Please, go away. And cancel the jab. I don't want it any more.' The girl disappeared back up the stairs and Kelly wondered if she should follow. But deciding that in the frame of mind her young patient was in, she would do more harm than good and she let herself out of the house.

Kelly glanced back at the tall, depressing building which years ago must have been quite beautiful. Now it looked bleak and uncared-for, which was not far off the condition of one of its residents, Kelly thought as she left reluctantly.

She had just nudged the front of her car onto the road when she heard a police siren. A white and blue car sped out of the drive on the opposite side of the road and was followed by a dark green saloon that paused before following it. To Kelly's surprise, she saw it was Marco at the wheel as he raised his hand in recognition. A few seconds later he swung the car up onto the pavement and jumped out.

'Kelly, what are you doing here?' he asked as he sprinted across the road to reach her, leaning down to her open window. He was dressed in casual light grey trousers and a soft linen shirt that made him look tall and leanly elegant. The familiar tangy, fruity aroma of aftershave blew off his skin on the morning breeze and melted into the air around her.

'Just a house call,' she replied, her eyes going to the opening in the laurel-lined drive opposite. 'And you?'

'We had a call from the police. They have just arrested a young man who is registered as our patient. They wanted—amongst other things—to know if he is receiving prescription drugs. I referred them to Jamie, of course.'

'And he lives over there?'

He nodded. 'It's a large house converted to flats…' His eyes rose to the building behind her. 'Very similar to the one you have just left. This young man tried to drive his motorbike through bushes at the back of the house and caused himself and the property some damage. It was only superficial, but it was necessary to examine him before they took him into custody.'

Kelly nodded thoughtfully. There was no reason, other than the mention of a motorbike, to suspect this had anything to do with Tania. Yet she couldn't help but draw a link.

'I'll meet you back at the surgery?' he said, a flash of white teeth against sun-bronzed skin making her forget briefly Tania Farlow's bruised face. But as she drove behind the dark green saloon, the image returned to her and Kelly wondered if it was possible her young patient was connected with the man who had just been arrested.

Marco climbed out of his car as she drove into the practice car park. He waited as she locked her vehicle and they walked together towards the practice in the warm, hazy heat of the morning. Marco's arm briefly touched hers and she felt the strange yet familiar curl of excitement in her stomach.

'Your patient,' he asked suddenly, 'was not one that we visited together?'

She gazed up at him, idly wondering if the bold, straight nose and sculpted bone structure were inherited from his father or mother and whether all five of the Dallori brothers possessed as much charm and allure as Marco himself. If so, she thought wryly, it seemed almost unfair that one family contained so much testosterone. 'No,' she answered, dragging back her thoughts with difficulty. 'She's a student, and was due for a meningitis jab but didn't show up for her appointment.'

'And you thought it necessary to call?'

'Since I ordered the vaccine especially—yes. She didn't respond to phone enquiries, so I thought the best thing to do was to call.'

'But all was not well?' he asked curiously.

'No, she looked dreadful. Swollen eye, facial bruising and she seemed very nervous. She told me she'd fallen off her boyfriend's motorbike.'

'And you didn't believe her?'

'Not sure, really. Her flatmate said she'd had an argument with her boyfriend. Then when you mentioned the young man and his motorbike…'

'You think he may be the boyfriend.' He nodded. 'It's possible.'

She smiled, her violet eyes catching the light of the sun. 'I'm probably way off the mark. But she *was* frightened. And if drugs are involved…'

He frowned, a wing of thick, raven-black hair curving across his forehead. 'As I told you, I was asked to make certain he was not injured, which he wasn't, except for several scratches to his face that looked rather inflamed. They were some hours old, with the blood dried around them. He lied, explaining the cuts were due to the bushes he drove through.'

'Could they have been fingernail scratches?'

'Indeed.'

Kelly sighed. 'Well, I've nothing to go on. Just a hunch.'

He grinned. 'A hunch is your best—what do you call it, *radar*?'

She laughed softly. 'Yes, I suppose so. But gut feeling isn't exactly a precise science.'

He ran long, tanned his fingers over his jaw. 'Will your young student be receptive to help?'

Kelly shook her head. 'She wasn't this morning. But maybe later, when she's had time to think.'

'Well, if I can be of help, please, let me know.'

Kelly smiled. 'Thanks.' She was about to move on, but then she paused. 'How are Frederico and Isabella?'

His eyes danced teasingly. 'Frederico is having lessons with a tutor. Isabella is attending the college.' His gaze deepened to a rich, ocean blue and she felt heat flood over her face. 'As for me—though you did not ask—I have missed our time together.'

His eyes flowed hungrily over her, their centers like tiny lasers boring into her soul as her heart twisted in response as she gazed into the gorgeous blue pools that were threatening to make her go back on her vow.

But sanity returned just in time as she forced her legs to move toward the practice. 'I think we had better go in,' she aid in a shaky whisper as he accompanied her in silence, he air filled with a crackling intensity that had her quick-ening her pace almost to a run.

Reception was bustling with patients. A line snaked in a disorderly way from the desk and only the tops of the re-ceptionists' heads were visible while Sam and Becky, the practice nurses, tried to field the arrival of latecomers.

'It seems we shall be parted yet again,' Marco whispered as they made their way through the waiting room and into the hall, and she glanced up into the sparkling, teasing gaze that held hers.

She found herself smiling and she wondered if he ever grew angry or irritated or even a little ruffled. He seemed so calm, so certain of himself, and maybe that was part of the incredible attraction.

It was too complicated to work out, she realized, and with a light-hearted smile, which she hoped hid all her in-ternal confusion, she flew to her room. This man had crept under her skin. She had tried her hardest to draw an emo-tional line between them, but every time she thought she had succeeded, she only had to look into his eyes to know she had failed. He knew it, too. He knew it and yet he was deliberately keeping his distance as he had promised her.

She couldn't fault him on that. Oh, no. He hadn't over-stepped the mark in any way, but, then, he didn't need to. He was in her mind and her thoughts already. He was in her head. She could hear his deep, sexy voice and smell the scent that made shivers tingle over every inch of skin. He was as tangible when he wasn't there as when he was.

And the awful thing was, she knew the torture wasn't going to stop.

As she went to the little mirror above the handbasin, the reflection she saw seemed to mock her. Silky dark hair curved around large, questioning indigo eyes. Not the expression of a confident thirty-year-old. More like an uncertain sixteen-year-old.

This man was haunting her. And she simply didn't know how to exorcise him.

Kelly had always loved Saturdays at the marina. From the first weekend she had moved there, a sense of excitement had swept up the small but enthusiastic sailing fraternity. They were a lively lot and irrespective of the weather, worked or relaxed on their craft.

Kelly had sailed with her sister, Meg, when they'd been children. Their mother had just managed to afford the holidays that provided her two girls with the opportunity to discover somewhere other than the Midlands. And Kelly knew that every penny had been saved for their benefit.

As Kelly watched the brightly coloured boats glide in and out of the marina, she wondered if Meg, now living in Paris with her French husband and two children, indulged in their shared passion.

Meg had been in her mind a lot lately. She hadn't phoned France since before she'd begun at Charbourne. A smile touched Kelly's full mouth as she gazed out from her large lounge picture window. She really should do it today...

But, as always, there seemed a hundred and one other things that took priority. Shopping, filling the freezer, a game of squash at the club that she had postponed that night she had called on Marco...

Kelly padded back across the floor in her mules, ambling luxuriously through her wide and spacious lounge to the kitchen. She felt lazy and hungry and made herself a breakfast of fresh fruit and toast and took it outside to her little lawn. The square of grass was enough to sunbathe on and the tall pine fence that surrounded it afforded perfect privacy.

It wasn't a patch on number one twenty-two East Side, she thought dryly as she sipped juice and ate her meal under the canopy of an umbrella. Marco had leased a property that was way out of her league.

But, then, he had a young son and niece to cater for. One thought led to another as she reclined back in her padded chair and smoothed protective sunscreen onto her skin. What was Marco doing today? Probably swimming first thing in the pool and maybe eating breakfast as she was, relaxing in the early morning sunshine.

He wasn't on call, so he'd have the day to do with as he wished. Maybe he would take Frederico and Isabella out. To the sea? The beaches? The harbour? Or maybe a run in the country...

Kelly closed her eyes and lay back as the sun warmed her long, bare legs. Why was it she couldn't stop thinking about Marco? The taunting little voice inside wouldn't leave her alone. She could be with them. She could be part of today, enjoying a wonderful Saturday that in reality she had no real plans to fill.

Kelly sat up, cross with herself. She smoothed down her shorts and lowered her legs to the ground, pushing her feet into mules. A few minutes later she had found her sports bag and packed swimming gear. There were a zillion things she wanted to do. First, a swim at the sports club in the open-air pool. Thirty challenging lengths should soon take her mind off Marco Dallori.

A few seconds later she was locking up and making her way to the garage. Her sunhat flapped in the breeze and one hand went up to secure it as she flipped the opening device of the automatic door. A twinge of guilt made her pause. Really, she should walk. The club wasn't far away, but she might go into town afterwards and do a little shopping.

Something caught her eye then, a small figure sitting on the edge of a pontoon. Dressed in light blue shorts and a T-shirt, the dark-headed boy was absorbed in watching the boats.

Was it Frederico?

Slowly she began to walk towards the road and the grass verge that bordered the water. The boy appeared to have his feet dangling over the side as he watched some other children on a nearby boat.

'Frederico?' she called, and he turned and recognized her at once, jumping up and almost leaping into her arms. She couldn't understand a word he was saying.

'That was a nice welcome.' She grinned and hugged him as he talked rapidly in Italian, but she only just managed to make out Isabella's name.

'All right, don't worry, I'll phone Papa,' she said, and he grasped her hand, his small, firm fingers winding round hers as they walked back to her apartment. Once they were inside, she took him into the kitchen and made a drink. The problem of communication was solved as she poured him a hefty helping of cornflakes and milk and he ate it hungrily.

'I'm going to telephone your father,' she said slowly, forming the words carefully so that he understood. 'Look, I'll put on the TV.' She pointed to the portable set on the worktop and flipped it on, leaving him eating and watching noisy cartoon characters as she went into the hall to dial Marco's number. He answered immediately.

'Marco, it's Kelly. I've Frederico with me.' She added quickly, 'He's absolutely fine.'

The pause before he replied was enough to confirm her fears that he had been missing his son. 'Thank God, Kelly. Where did you find him?'

'Close to my apartment. He said something about Isabella—I'm afraid I didn't quite understand what he was trying to tell me.'

'Yes, they went to the marina boating shop. Isabella met a friend from college. Frederico must have wandered off while they were talking.'

'The boating shop is just around the corner. He hadn't gone far.'

'But to leave her, when he knows that he should never stray from her side!' Marco stopped and cleared his throat. 'I'm sorry. It's just that we have been so worried.'

'How long has he been lost?'

'Not long, fortunately. Isabella returned a short while ago, expecting to find him here. We were just considering what to do next.'

'He obviously lost track of time and place,' Kelly suggested gently, aware of how concerned he must be. 'I'm sure he wouldn't have gone far.'

'Can I come and collect him?'

'Of course.' She added lightly, 'Coffee's on.'

When she got back to the kitchen, Frederico had his elbows propped on the bar, his attention riveted to the TV. Kelly perched on a stool beside him and, as she waited for Marco, lost herself in the addictive sensation of a warm little body snuggling closely against her.

Kelly watched father and son embrace a few minutes later, unable to repress the pang of envy that curled round her ribs. The little boy was so loving and uninhibited. Marco, too, was unafraid to show his relief and joy as he hunkered down, his powerful arms encircling the little figure.

Conversing rapidly in their native tongue, the problem seemed quickly resolved to Marco's satisfaction as he nodded patiently, listening as Frederico almost ran out of breath in his eagerness to explain.

At last Marco lifted two large but gentle hands and cupped the tanned cheeks and deep brown eyes that gazed anxiously back at him. '*Si, si*,' he interrupted with a grin that stated plainly he understood. '*Non importa*, Frederico.'

Kelly saw the relief spread over his son's face and Marco laughed softly, ruffling the cap of deep black hair. 'Now we must speak in English,' he said more firmly as he rose to his feet. 'I think you have something to say to Dr Anders.'

Frederico turned to her, mirroring his father's expression. 'Thank you, Dr Anders.'

Her heart gave a little tug as she smiled. 'You're welcome, Frederico.'

'While Isabelle was talking to her friend, Frederico went to look at the model boats on display in another part of the shop,' Marco explained. 'On his return, Isabelle had disappeared. Assuming she had left for the apartment, Frederico followed but lost his way. He said he was trying to think what to do when you found him.'

Kelly nodded. 'Very sensibly he hadn't wandered far.'

'And I understand his breakfast was delicious.' Marco's blue eyes twinkled. 'Now we must allow you to catch up on your morning.'

Kelly felt an unreasonable stab of disappointment as Marco reached out a hand to his son. Frederico glanced up at her as they moved to the front door, then tugged at Marco's arm.

'*Per favore*—please, Papa!'

Marco paused. 'No, Frederico.'

'What is it?' Kelly asked as Frederico's dark brown eyes held hers.

Marco sighed. 'It is nothing.'

'Please, Papa,' Frederico said urgently, tugging his father's hand once more.

'I think you'd better tell me.' Kelly shrugged.

Marco stood hesitantly, his long lashes sweeping down on his cheeks, obviously considering what to do. But finally he gave a rueful smile. 'My son has asked if you would consider having lunch with us.' He curled an eyebrow upward. 'I'm sorry. But you did ask.'

Frederico came to stand beside her, his eyes fiercely expectant. How in the world was she going to refuse him? She looked to Marco for help but she could see that she wasn't going to get any. The two Dallori males were exerting what had to be a unique and very powerful charisma that left her feeling as though she had virtually no willpower at all.

A little sigh escaped her lips as she looked into Frederico's imploring face and gave up any hope of refusing.

*   *   *

They ate al fresco on the terrace of Marco's apartment, a light lunch of salad and cold meats and twists of freshly baked bread from the marina bakery. The crisis of the morning over, Isabella and Frederico played in the pool while Kelly and Marco sat under the large white canvas umbrella.

Marco stretched out on the cushioned seat, wearing pale knee-length cotton shorts and a black short-sleeved shirt. Light Indian thongs hung from his feet as he crossed one bronzed leg over the other, a pair of sunglasses resting on his aquiline nose. Kelly was acutely aware of him beside her as their arms lay on the armrests of the seats, only inches apart.

She had quickly changed her shorts before leaving her apartment, swapping them for a pair of new denim shorts and a white vest top that were more suited to the occasion. Her long legs were stretched out, her feet shoeless, a pair of summer sandals deposited by the side of her lounger. She was trying to relax or at least look relaxed as she sipped the long fruit drinks that Isabella had made and brought to them.

But Marco's presence was too distracting to really feel comfortable and every now and then she would catch herself glancing from the corner of her eye at his long, resting form, reminding her how infrequently she had allowed herself to be close to him.

Not that he seemed altogether contained himself. She noticed a little muscle flexing in his jaw, as though he, too, was finding the intimacy of sitting so closely with the invisible vibrations between them far too strong to discount, more than he had bargained for as he had suggested they relax there.

Then suddenly he turned to her, removing his sunglasses and fixing her with that intense blue stare that melted like hot ice over her skin. He raised his voice over the laughter and splashing from the pool, his smooth forehead drawing into a pleat. 'Kelly, have you any plans for the rest of the day?'

As always he took her by surprise and she brought her hand up to curl the wing of silky brown hair behind her ear, adjusting her own sunglasses as she did so. 'I had nothing specific in mind.'

'In that case, I should value your opinion on a matter I must attend to for my brother and sister-in-law,' he interrupted quickly. 'Their house—Canzone del Mare—is being redecorated before their return. I must check it out to make certain things are going according to plan.'

'But surely you won't need me—' she began, only to be stopped by a smile that was almost dazzling.

'You are just the person, in fact. Laura has asked me to have a small pond created below the lounge window. I have no idea what a woman would like to see as she gazes out—perhaps you could tell me.'

Kelly smiled ruefully. 'Hasn't Laura indicated what she'd like?'

'This is to be a surprise. I would be most grateful if you could help.'

Kelly looked back at Frederico bouncing off the slide and into the water, his brown little body clad in white swimming shorts. He caught her eye as he bobbed above the surface and waved. She waved back then looked at Marco. 'Well, if I really can be of use…'

'I am in your debt,' he murmured, his beautiful eyes tangling seductively with hers as he rose to his feet, holding out his hands to help her up.

CHAPTER FOUR

SHE wouldn't be sitting in the car—alone with Marco, Kelly reflected dryly, if she had known Isabella and Frederico were going out for the afternoon. Apparently it was a prior arrangement with Isabella's Italian friend from the language college, who had suggested they take Frederico to the sports club for the afternoon.

Now Kelly sat beside Marco as he drove them along the steep hill road towards the cliffs and Antonio's house. 'I didn't realize there would be just the two of us,' she mused as she relaxed, a little unwillingly, on the cool, expensive leather of the luxurious car.

'Does that worry you?' He couldn't suppress the amusement in his voice.

'No, why should it?' she answered a little defensively. 'It's just that…well, aren't you worried that Frederico might wander off again?'

'Not really.' He shrugged, slipping the wheel casually through beautifully shaped fingers. 'I am satisfied this morning was just a silly mistake. Now, sit back and relax. I promise to get you back home before nightfall.'

'That's a relief.' Kelly grinned and met his eyes for one teasing moment before gazing back at the clear stretch of blue sea and sky that looked almost transparent in the heat of the afternoon.

It was a glorious day. A little wind ruffled the tufts of green grass that dotted the fenced barriers of the cliffs and gulls wheeled overhead, their strange cackles sounding like laughter through the open roof of the car. She wasn't quite sure where the afternoon was going, only that she was enjoying the moment and the weird sensation of feeling how right it felt just to be sitting next to him.

The cliff road straightened out and Marco turned down a lane that bordered a fringe of pretty houses. Palm trees and tropical plants grew in abundance and red, pink, orange and yellow flowers tumbled over their walls.

But Kelly wasn't prepared for the sight of the stunning white house that stood at the end of the lane slightly apart from all the rest. Its stucco walls and shuttered half-moon windows looked more in keeping with a Mediterranean villa, though much of the house was hidden by scaffolding.

Marco drove through the wrought-iron gates and up the long sandy drive, parking outside the heavy oak front door.

'So this is your brother's house,' Kelly said in awe, as she climbed out and stood for a moment, shielding her eyes from the glare as the sun hit the pure white walls. 'What did you say its name was?'

'Canzone del Mare,' Marco murmured as he came to stand beside her. 'It means song of the sea. Let me show you the interior. I apologize in advance for the dust. It is everywhere, I am afraid.'

'What is your brother having done?' Kelly asked as he led her up the steps and turned a key in the heavy brass lock.

'The roof requires special treatment that will preserve the cinnamon-coloured tiles. They have one little girl, Maria, and they hope to have more children so an extension is being built on, too.'

Marco led the way through the house. Though all the furniture had been removed, the workmen had placed dust-sheets over the marble floor tiles that ran through the house. The impression of light and space was dominant and Kelly could imagine what a stunning home it would make when complete.

Marco unlocked one of the ocean-facing windows and they walked out onto the terrace. Charbourne Bay glistened in the sunshine as an array of coloured craft bobbed up and down on the blue water.

'Stunning, isn't it?' Marco leaned his tanned arms on the wall and gazed out to sea.

Kelly inhaled slowly. 'Beautiful.'

'Antonio designed it to resemble our family home in Capri, also called Canzone del Mare.'

Kelly drew in a sigh, closing her violet eyes. Salt air flowed into her lungs and she held its freshness for a few seconds before exhaling. Even with her eyes shut she could feel his presence and sense his eyes resting on her.

'Does your mother live there?' she asked as she opened them, imagining the Dallori family home in her mind. Marco had drawn a very clear picture for her and now, standing here in the sunshine which was as warm as any Italian sun, she felt strangely transported.

'Mamma lives there now, yes, though before my father's death she travelled with him all over the world. They even had a house built in Surrey, so that Papa could commute to London in his work as a surgeon.'

'Has your mother kept that house on?' Kelly asked curiously.

'No, it now belongs to my uncle.' Marco's eyes flickered softly. 'After my father's heart attack, Mamma wanted only to be in Capri. Her real life is there, with her grandchildren. Though now, of course, she will travel frequently to England to visit Antonio and Laura.'

For a while they remained silent, absorbed in thought as they looked out to sea. Kelly felt a brief pang of envy for Laura, who had seemed so effortlessly to have made the transition from one culture to another and become part of this close, warm Italian family.

She could understand the attraction that Laura must have felt for Antonio. With Marco standing as close as he was, it was difficult to stop her pulse from rocketing and her heart from thudding under her ribs. The tension in the air grew stronger as he moved beside her, his elbows propped on the stone of the balcony and his shoulder touching hers.

'And you, Kelly, what of your family?' he asked softly, as the sun lit up her soft, creamy complexion and high-lighted the swirls of navy blue in her huge violet eyes. She tried not to be distracted by the sensual, hungry mouth and dark features that were so uniquely Latin as she inhaled the musky scent that drifted off his hot skin.

'There's not much to tell.' She shrugged indifferently. 'I've one sister—Meg. We grew up in the Midlands, left home for university—and when Mum died, we drifted really. Meg met the love of her life in Paris when she was working as a translator. They married and moved to Paris and now have two adorable children.'

'And your father?' Marco prompted, and Kelly swallowed. For a reason that she couldn't explain she found herself telling him how, when she'd been fourteen, her father had simply not come home one day.

'He disappeared?' Marco asked incredulously.

Kelly nodded. 'Dad worked for an oil company and we thought maybe his flight had been cancelled from the Middle East. Mum checked and his plane landed, but he didn't turn up.'

'What about his firm or the police?'

'Mum approached them, of course. For weeks we thought he would show up. Mum didn't sleep or eat. She lived by the phone, but it never rang—until it was too late.' Kelly pushed back the feelings that she held tightly in check for so many years. 'Meg took the call. It was after Mum's funeral. It was Dad and he said he was sorry to hear that she'd died. That the longer it had gone on, he said, the more difficult it had been to get in contact with us. He flew over to meet us a few weeks later with his partner and their two children.' She bit her lip. 'It was weird. We knew him and yet we didn't.'

Marco paused, frowning. 'Do you keep in contact?'

'Yes, we write or phone from time to time. Enough to

be civilized.' She shrugged. 'I don't think we'll ever know the real reason why he left us. He said it was because he couldn't bring himself to tell Mum that the marriage was over. And the longer he stayed away, the more difficult it was to make contact.'

'Perhaps it was best your mother never knew,' he murmured gently.

'Perhaps.' Kelly looked up at him. 'Do you know, I can't remember ever having seen her wearing something new. I thought of it a little while ago and realized how much she'd sacrificed to get Meg and I through university.'

'She wanted only the best for you.'

Kelly blinked, suddenly aware of his eyes focused on her. 'I'm sorry. You must be bored. I don't know why I'm telling you all this.'

'Because I asked you. Because I am interested.'

'Well,' she said lightly, 'I can't think why.'

'Can't you?' There was a softness in his bone structure that added to the flare of tender deep blue in his eyes. 'I am interested in everything about you, Kelly Anders.'

Her heart seemed to go crazy. Amazement filled her as she read those expressively intense pools of turquoise that gazed down above prominent, classical cheekbones that looked sculptured from golden stone. Breathlessly she gazed up, frightened and excited all at once, part of her wanting to acknowledge the message that was clearly relayed in their depths as though he knew words would frighten her too much.

But the other part of her, the focused, logical, practical part of Kelly Anders, and usually the dominant side of her character, was shouting out that she was about to dive into waters that were far too dangerous to swim in.

'I think we should be talking about your sister-in-law's pond,' Kelly said quickly, tearing away her hypnotized gaze. She couldn't see his expression but she could feel his disappointment with every particle of her being as she turned, wondering which way they were to go.

'Below the lounge window,' he said quietly, taking her arm. 'Follow the path at the side of the house.'

She nodded, aware of the gentle pressure of his fingers as they followed the path that led to the rear gardens. Here, the sun fell over the long lawn that rolled down to a copse of young trees. The house looked even more beautiful from this point, Kelly thought as she gazed up at it, despite the ugly poles and scaffolding in place around the white walls.

'There is the lounge,' Marco said, pointing to a window above a flower-filled dip in the lawn.

'And just below it, a perfect place for a pond,' Kelly decided. 'With a fountain and a few wooden windchimes. Even a little bridge across it with an oriental flavour.'

'And a pagoda.' Marco nodded as they moved slowly up the soft green lawn.

She laughed softly as the tension between them eased. 'You see, it's done already.'

'With your help,' he murmured as suddenly he seemed very close again. Though he wasn't actually touching her, the proximity of his lean, powerful body sent a surge of heat upward to her face. Her instinct was to step back and give herself space to breathe as her lungs fought for air, but her legs felt almost paralysed and she stood still, feeling as though he could sense every thought in her head.

'It…it's such a lovely garden,' she flustered as his gaze flowed down on her, feeling as hot and sensuous as the warm, sultry sun overhead.

'Perfect for a family.' He nodded. 'I am sure my brother and his wife will spend many happy years here.'

Kelly was sure they would, too, and again part of her yearned for that close-knit family relationship that had been absent in her own and Meg's lives. Perhaps she could have had something close to it with Tim, but their relationship had never held the spark that she knew was needed to ignite the fire that lay unfanned deep inside her.

'And what is your vision for the future?' Marco asked, almost stealing the thoughts out of her head and she looked up into the astute deep blue gaze. 'Have you ever considered marriage and a family?'

The garden seemed suddenly very quiet and all she could hear was Marco's soft breathing and her own heartbeat, which was struggling in vain to regain its steadiness under the laser-like focus of the man standing beside her.

'Once,' she admitted, wondering why she was answering so truthfully when, with a little ingenuity, she could have shrugged the question aside. 'A long time ago, when I was training. He was a truly nice guy. Too nice perhaps.'

Marco waited, his gaze searching her face. 'Is that possible?'

'Oh, yes.' Kelly folded her arms about her, feeling chilly in her vest top and shorts as the shadows slowly made their way across the lawn. 'Tim wanted the whole package. Two point four kids, a house and a mortgage...'

'And you did not,' he supplied for her.

She paused. 'Not then, no.'

'And now?'

She looked up at him and felt a shiver of awareness crackle down her back. 'I've never met anyone since Tim...anyone whom I felt...comfortable enough with to even visualize a future.'

He gave a strange little smile. 'You intrigue me, Kelly.'

'Do I?' She smiled shakily. 'I can't see why.'

'You don't feel the need to share your life with someone?'

Kelly trapped her lip. Where was this conversation leading? She had already said too much about herself and why should he be that interested anyway? 'I know it sounds like a cliché, Marco, but I love my work. I really do. And I wouldn't want to jeopardize it by dividing myself into lots of separate emotional pieces. I've had friends who thought they could combine a demanding career with just as much of a demanding relationship. And they've fallen at the first fence.'

'So you believe that loving your work precludes you from loving a man?'

'No,' she bit back quickly. 'Of course not. I didn't say that.'

'I am glad to hear it.'

'Now you're teasing me.'

He lifted an eyebrow. 'Do you object?'

'To you teasing me?' She laughed. 'Actually, no. It's very flattering to be teased at thirty.'

'Then I shall flatter you more.' His grin widened and a white glint of teeth sparkled through his parted lips. 'Maybe I shall even tease you about marriage.'

'Marriage?' She laughed embarrassedly. 'That's a long way down the line. Too far for me even to imagine. And if I don't ever meet the love of my life—'

'You will be content without love?' he interrupted ruefully as his body brushed against hers and his breath fanned softly down on her cheeks.

Kelly felt her body tremble. Perhaps it was the unbelievably intoxicating scent that flowed off his skin and made her insides curl that had such an effect, or maybe it was the way his full, wide mouth opened so expressively, parted in a question that she had no hope of answering.

Whatever it was, she suppressed the almost overpowering urge to place her hands on Marco's wide shoulders and, here in the fantasy garden of her dreams, slide her fingers slowly around his neck and let her body curve naturally into his. The silence smouldered between them, her eyes locked to his, a breathless hush still hanging in the summer air.

For a moment Kelly thought he was about to bend his head a fraction closer, and from there it would take one small movement on her part to lift her head slightly. His lips were still parted, their soft, silky surface glimmering in the sun and contrasting against the dark, grainy texture of his skin. She felt transfixed, caught in a moment of time

as though she had opened her innermost self up to his gaze
and her soul was at risk of being devoured.

Then suddenly there was an almighty crash behind them
and they almost sprang apart. Marco was the first to turn
swiftly on his heel and look up, shading his eyes as he
frowned up at the house.

'The workmen have arrived back from lunch,' he said
abruptly, nodding to a small group of men wearing hard
yellow hats climbing up the ladders attached to the scaffolding.

'Yes,' she agreed, swallowing quickly. 'So they have.'

'I am afraid our quiet afternoon will be disturbed.'

'At least we discussed the pond,' she said, her voice
sounding as weak as her legs felt. 'And you'll have some
ideas to offer your sister-in-law.'

'She will be very grateful,' he said, and she smiled, hauling in her shattered senses as he slipped a hand around her
waist and guided her back up the slope and to his car.

Marco flipped on a CD as they drove home and so removed the need for either of them to converse. A beautiful
soprano voice filled the air and Kelly tried not to let her
thoughts wander back to what had happened at Canzone.

It was only when Marco pulled up outside her apartment
that she turned to look at him, uncertain as to his reaction.
But she needn't have been concerned because he had
slipped on his sunglasses and his smile was back in place.

The evening sun was shimmering low in the sky as he
escorted her up the path to her apartment. Suddenly Kelly
didn't want to go in. She wanted to stay with him, be in
his company and talk for hours—about anything and everything.

But that was too ridiculous for words, she realized. He
had a family to go home to and if he had wanted her company then he would have asked. Disappointment filled her
as they stood outside, and to hide it she busied herself with
searching for her keys in her bag.

'Thank you for accompanying me today,' he said in a

husky voice, and she smiled, looking up to find his eyes softly on her.

'It was lovely,' she murmured. 'I enjoyed visiting Canzone.'

'It is a beautiful house.'

She nodded. 'Very beautiful.'

He looked at her steadily. 'As is the woman who shared it with me this afternoon.' He was only teasing, but she felt her cheeks heat all the same, yet before she could make light of his flattery he added quickly, 'Kelly, this afternoon we have begun to know one another a little more, no? Now, I think, you can trust me.'

How did he know that she hadn't trusted him? How could he have possibly read her mind? Had it shown on her face from that very first day when she had suspected that he was acting for Antonio?

And did she still believe that Marco's interest in her was linked to her role at the practice? The answer to that, she realized, was no.

'We have made a big step forward,' he murmured, in the absence of her reply, reaching out to take her hand in his as her heart pounded wildly inside her chest. Then he bent slowly and pressed his lips in a slow kiss against her cheek, her lashes flying down to flutter in shocked acknowledgement. For a few seconds his arm went around her waist and he held her, his breath flowing over her skin in a shallow wave, and then as suddenly he released her.

'*Buona sera*, Kelly,' he murmured, his eyes flaring like shooting stars on a summer night. Then he turned, his tall, broad-shouldered frame moving down the path, leaving her shakily berating herself for not offering him coffee, in the same second knowing precisely why.

It was a whole week before Kelly gave in.

Not that Marco made it difficult for her—on the contrary. He was his usual friendly, smiling self and, providing she didn't allow herself to gaze into his eyes for longer than was absolutely necessary, she managed to handle their meetings at work. However, there was one temptation she simply couldn't resist.

The photographs.

Having learnt all she had from Marco about his family, a little voice inside her head kept asking why she did not access the Dallori archives! Easy enough, as Becky had suggested. But there was always someone in the staffroom when she was there, and she couldn't bring herself to open the cupboard and slide out the album.

She ignored the emotional itch for seven days, grateful for her busy days and nights of being on call, but on an overcast Monday evening in the middle of July, Kelly found herself working later than usual.

Her list had genuinely stretched to six-thirty. Then she had several house visits and, of course, she could have gone straight back to the marina. But she could also be super-efficient and return the records she had to the centre, thus leaving the next day with one less assignment.

Or at least, that was how she convinced herself. Feeling slightly less guilty at her secret mission, she sat at her desk in the deserted building and completed her duties. Not that procrastination—or guilt—helped, she admitted silently as she went upstairs to the staffroom.

She still had the feeling she was behaving like a voyeur as she almost tiptoed into the silent room. The magazines and piles of medical journals were spread over one of the worktops and a neat row of clean mugs stood by the electric kettle. On the far side of the room the cupboard beckoned her and, finally admitting defeat, she went to open it.

The large white album was there, as Becky had explained, resting on top of a pile of books. Kelly handled it almost reverently as she carried it to an easy chair and sat down, opening it slowly on her lap.

Kelly's eyes ran down the list of wonderful Italian names that graced the page in soft, flowing handwriting which she guessed must be Laura's. The photograph that followed was a glossy colour print of the bride and groom standing in front of the church door under a huge white fabric bow.

Antonio was tall, dark and imposingly handsome, while Laura was slender and exquisitely attired in her beautiful silk wedding dress. Kelly identified Maria, Laura's little girl, wreathed in smiles and a pretty white dress with a blue sash. She held tightly to an older woman's outstretched hand as they stood beside Laura.

They all looked deliriously happy. Laura gazed radiantly at the camera from under her fragile headdress and Antonio smiled the stunning Dallori smile. Kelly turned the page slowly, her intake of breath sharp as she saw the next photograph. The group had enlarged, for a man was now standing beside Antonio whom she recognized at once. Marco was slightly taller than his brother, looking devastatingly handsome in his morning suit, his thick, black hair curving gently to his collar and his beautiful eyes fixed steadily on the photographer's lens.

Kelly's heart beat faster. Her hand moved unconsciously to his image, her fingertips tracing his tall, erect shape as his eyes seemed to devour hers, their luminous depths shining out from his deeply tanned face. She remained for some while, sitting quietly, staring into them. Then when she felt she had drunk in every last drop of his essence, she turned the page.

Images met her eyes of the vast Italian family that Laura had married into. She gazed at all of them in turn, admiring the dazzling culture that produced such smooth Roman features and olive skins. All Marco's brothers were tall and handsome, standing beside their elegant wives and gorgeous children, their names carefully chronicled in the same flowing handwriting at the bottom of the page.

When at last she closed the album, Kelly sat back in her chair and closed her eyes. She felt as though she knew them all in a strange way. But the thought that was uppermost in her mind was that although Marco had appeared in many of the photographs, with Frederico standing at his side, the absence of a female partner had been noticeable.

Why had Marco never married again? she wondered as she placed the album carefully back in the cupboard and left the staffroom. Not that her little adventure into the Dallori archives had served to enlighten her, she decided as she drove home. If anything, the photographs in the album had only provided her with far more questions than answers.

CHAPTER FIVE

AS THE days passed, Kelly began to wonder if she had imagined that beautiful afternoon at Canzone. And thinking back to the kiss they had shared only made her wonder if Marco had been teasing her and the intimacy that she had assumed he had genuinely meant had been a spur-of-the-moment gesture and had meant little or nothing.

At work, he reacted as he did with any member of staff and part of her was relieved that he did so. The grapevine had cooled and even Becky's interest had waned. But the other part of her still held on to the ridiculous notion they had shared something special. She hadn't talked so openly about her father to anyone except Meg and the memories she had so carefully hidden away still stirred unrest.

She wondered how Meg felt about the past. Had she regrets that their father wasn't part of her life? Had what had happened when they had been children affected her relationship with Pierre? Living in different countries, they had never really talked about it after their mother had died.

It was a steamy, overcast afternoon late in July when Kelly scribbled a reminder on her pad to call Meg. Just as she was tucking the pad into her bag, the phone rang.

'Kelly, it's Marco. I'm at the police station.' He paused. 'Did you see your young patient again, the one who missed her meningitis jab?'

'No—why?' Kelly asked, sitting up.

'A young woman was attacked yesterday—in that road.'

'You don't think it's Tania?'

'There's no information yet—and I have not mentioned the connection.'

Kelly glanced at her watch. 'As soon as I'm finished, I'll drive over there.'

'Don't go alone,' Marco warned. 'I'll come with you.'

Could it possibly be Tania? Kelly wondered as she saw her next two patients, wishing that she had done more to reach the girl on her last visit. Yet what more could she have done other than to hammer on the door and make a nuisance of herself? Which, in the long run, would probably have only alienated her more.

Nevertheless, Marco's call filled her with a strong sense of foreboding and, after completing a repeat prescription for her last patient, she dashed to the cloakroom, splashed cool water on her face and ran a brush through her hair.

Marco had arrived by the time she returned and he looked a little preoccupied, his black hair falling across his forehead as he stood waiting for her. But his smile was as heart-stopping as ever and it was a few moments before Kelly finally tuned in as he told her what had happened at the police station.

'The man I was called to examine today,' he said as he sat down, his broad shoulders rising in a shrug under the crisp white shirt, 'had been arrested for burglary. Because he had been in custody overnight, he appeared to be in withdrawal. Drugs were found on him, but he insisted he was not the dealer and that he had bought them from someone he knew only as Garry. It was then that I recognized the address—the youth with the motorbike.'

'But I thought he'd been arrested,' Kelly said anxiously.

'There was not enough evidence to press charges.' He frowned, rising slowly to his feet. 'We must not jump to conclusions but it will be wise to check.'

She was so glad he was with her, Kelly thought as he drove them to the depressing building where Tania lived. It looked bleaker than ever when they arrived, and even before Kelly climbed out of the car and pressed the door-bell, she had the feeling no one would answer.

'Someone must be in,' she persisted as she pressed again and Marco tried the locked door.

Just then a window opened above them and Kelly recognized the girl who looked out. 'If you want Tania, she's not here,' Tania's flatmate called, and Kelly stepped back, shielding her eyes from the sun as she looked up.

'Where can I find her?'

'Who's that with you?' She nodded suspiciously at Marco.

'He's a colleague and a friend, and we only want to help Tania—'

'It's a bit late for that,' the girl interrupted as the window closed with a bang. But a few seconds later the front door opened and she glared angrily at them from under her untidy dark hair. 'Tania's in hospital.'

'What happened?' Marco asked calmly as Kelly felt her stomach turn.

'She was beaten up and she's scared stiff of who did it to her.'

'Would that person be someone called Garry?' Marco asked, and Kelly could see that Tania's friend was shocked as she stood there, her eyes flying open.

'How do you know that?'

'It doesn't matter.' Marco shrugged. 'Have you told the police what you know?'

'Of course I haven't. I don't want to get involved. Tania should have got out of that relationship a long time ago, but when she got preg—' The girl stopped, biting her lip. 'I've said all I'm going to say. If you want to know any more, you'd better ask Tania.'

The door closed sharply and Kelly sighed. 'It's worse than I thought.'

Marco nodded. 'Yes, it appears so. Your young patient is pregnant.'

She nodded. 'I'd like to try the hospital next.'

'Of course.'

Kelly turned away from the house, aware of the strong hand resting supportively on her back.

Tania Farlow was in a side ward and the sister informed them that she was very tired and had been interviewed by the police earlier in the day.

Kelly feared that Tania wouldn't want to talk, but the sister reappeared with a brief nod. 'She'll see you.'

'Can you tell us anything about her injuries?' Kelly asked quickly, knowing that she probably wouldn't get much detail but she trying anyway.

'The obvious are wrist and rib fractures,' Sister said with expressively raised brows, 'but emotionally, she's in a state of shock.' She paused. 'We do expect her to make a full recovery. At least, physically.'

Tania lay in a hospital gown on the top of her bed. She looked pale and her arm was in plaster. She tried to sit up, obviously in pain, but Kelly shook her head. 'Lie still, Tania. We won't keep you long.' Kelly smiled, seating herself in the chair beside the bed.

'How did you know I was here?'

'We've just been to your flat and we spoke to your friend.' Kelly nodded to Marco. 'This is Dr Dallori, my colleague at the centre.'

Marco smiled and Tania flushed a little. 'What did she say?'

'Just that you were here.' Kelly frowned. 'What happened, Tania?'

'I can't tell you anything,' she replied nervously. 'I know you mean well, but I can't.'

'Because you're frightened of someone called Garry?' Marco perched on the end of the bed, his dark head inclined as he spoke.

'How...how did you know?' Tania looked as though she wanted to jump out of bed and run away, but Marco told her about his involvement and the events at the police station and she sank back on the pillow with a sigh.

'He said he'd kill me if I told the police,' she whispered

as she wiped her eyes with a tissue. 'I miscarried the baby...it was his and he didn't care...' She burst into tears and Kelly reached out to comfort her.

'Is that why when you came to me,' Kelly asked gently, 'you were uncertain about the meningitis immunization? Did you think you were pregnant?'

'I'd missed a period. I wasn't sure. I can't believe I let him...' She swallowed, staring through swollen eyes. 'He was so nice when I first met him. I really thought...' She sniffed, lifting her thin shoulders in a helpless shrug. 'What I thought and what he turned out to be were entirely different. He's only interested in one thing and that's making people do what he wants. Lyn warned me. I should have listened to her.'

Marco glanced at Kelly, then said softly, 'What does he want you to do, Tania?'

She tightened her mouth and looked away. 'He wants to use me. As a way of getting to get to know other first-year students.'

'To sell drugs?'

Tania nodded. 'He knows some of them have wealthy parents. They can get the money easily once they're hooked.'

'Have your parents any idea of what's happening?' Kelly asked.

'No, and I don't want them to know. I don't want to involve them. They're good people but not rich. They worked hard for my education. I don't want to disappoint them.'

'How did you get involved with Garry?'

'I used to see him on his motorbike. At first we just smiled. Then one day he asked me if I wanted a ride. After that, we went out and...and one thing led to another. I...I didn't know he was into drugs. Well, I knew he smoked a bit of pot. But when he tried to get me to take other stuff, I realized what he was doing.' Tania sniffed back the tears. 'I must have been crazy.'

'Have you told the police who did this to you?' Marco asked.

She looked terrified. 'No. Garry would kill me if I did.'

'He will go on doing this if he can get away with it,' Marco warned, his face tightening. 'The police need to know.'

'He just laughs at them,' Tania replied bitterly. 'Says they can't do anything.'

'A very pleasant character,' Marco said grimly. 'What will you do when you leave hospital?'

Tania shuddered. 'I don't know. But I can't stay in Charbourne.'

'But what about university,' Kelly protested, 'and your parents? What will you tell them?'

'That I had an accident,' Tania said, holding back a sob. 'And that I don't want to go back to studying.' She began weeping again and Kelly looked at Marco, who quietly raised his eyebrows.

Just then the sister entered and glanced at her watch, indicating it was time for them to leave. Kelly stood up and squeezed Tania's arm. 'Try to rest, Tania, and we'll talk again, OK?'

The girl nodded but Kelly knew as she left the little room what Tania would do. She had been through a nightmare and was still living in fear. There was no way she had the courage to do as Marco had suggested.

'Should *we* go to the police?' Kelly said as they drove back to the centre.

'We could.' Marco nodded, his face white with anger. 'But what can they do if she will not bring charges? They will ask her to make a statement against him. Almost certainly they will need corroboration from someone that she is not lying about the attack.'

'Lyn—her friend—knows all about him.'

'But she, too, is afraid, no?' He gave a little growl of anger.

'One day he must be caught,' Kelly sighed.

'And that day cannot come too soon,' Marco muttered, a muscle flexing in his jaw, tightening his features and hardening his profile in a way that Kelly had never seen before.

The moment came on Friday evening when Kelly found herself staring from her window, too tired to even think about what groceries to buy for the weekend. She had been on call since returning from the hospital—an unusual state of affairs, but Jamie had been down with a virus and Di Saunders was on holiday. Which had left only Liam and Marco for surgeries.

Not that the days had been furiously busy, thank God. But her nights had been interrupted and, come Friday at five, she was all in. If she'd had to face another duty night she would have had to prop matchsticks under her lids. But at short notice they had managed to initiate the deputizing service and now she could go home and crash.

A thought that was particularly appealing as she stifled a yawn and threaded a wing of glossy brown hair behind her ear. With a satisfied tap of a keyboard key, she logged off the system and listened to the energetic song of the birds in the sycamores outside.

She had just one fleeting regret. That she hadn't seen Marco all day—in fact, she hadn't seen much of him since the night they had visited Tania. She had been shocked at the degree of anger so clearly visible on his face. And it had been an abrupt goodbye, partly, she suspected, because he was holding himself in control.

But even then he'd summoned up a smile that had made her forget Tania briefly and her injuries, and how brutal human nature could be as he'd drifted a kiss across her cheek before she'd climbed out of his car.

But since then they had been so busy that a fleeting acknowledgement had been all they had made, and now Marco's car wasn't in the car park. So she wouldn't see him again until Monday and she felt ridiculously cheated.

Not that seeing him tonight would have made any difference. Two days stretched ahead with no contact, and why that should be such a hurdle, she didn't know. Except that their relationship had shifted yet again. She was beginning to feel she knew the man beneath the mask, the man who shielded his emotions with great skill. For that night, after seeing Tania, something in his face had touched her soul before he'd regained the composure that so rarely slipped.

Kelly sighed wistfully, a little frustrated with her pathetic attempt at understanding the man. She was no expert in that area, but she had always believed she had mastered a degree of human psychology. But whatever his history, which included the loss of his young wife, he didn't for one moment wear his heart on his sleeve.

Kelly lifted her bag and walked through to Reception. Julia Grey, the practice manager, said goodnight and Maggie Stevens, the secretary, sent her a little wave. But the phones were still ringing and Julia dashed a pile of papers into her arms and Kelly seized the opportunity to escape.

The evening was balmy and beautiful and, despite unbelievable weariness, Kelly inhaled joyously. Seaside summer nights were exquisite. The entire world seemed on holiday as the scents of the sea and sand and tourists mingled intoxicatingly.

It was the perfect evening for a stroll on the beach or a late swim. But there was only one place Kelly wanted to be. The shower that she had planned to soak under before falling into bed was calling and her tired body ached to heal under water.

She'd make do with bread and cheese and a little of the salad that surely was still surviving in the refrigerator salad box. And if it was past recognition, then she'd go for the pair of remaining eggs that had taunted her this morning and which she'd had no time to prepare for breakfast.

Then, just as she unlocked her car, she recognized the

sound of an engine purring into the car park. Her heart did a funny little turn that could mean only one thing. She turned and suddenly the tiredness fell away and, as if by magic, her world came back into focus.

Marco looked breathlessly handsome, despite the last two days of unending surgeries. His black hair tapered thickly down to his pale blue shirt collar, and as he bent to flick on the locking system of his car his broad shoulders strained under the soft material and the tanned muscles of his arms flexed powerfully with easy, economical strength. Then he straightened, sent her a smile to die for and walked towards her, his agile body covering the gravel path with casual strides.

She found everything about him sensual and sexy and yet he seemed so totally unaware of it. She knew she was utterly mad for thinking the way she was, but it was as if her mind had suddenly broken out of the barriers that had kept her grounded for too long after Tim.

'Hi, there,' he said, and leaned lazily against the car beside her. Marco looked so good she just wanted to slide her arms around him and lean into that chest and feel his solidness under her fingertips.

But wanting was one thing. Doing another. And even in her madness, she didn't have the courage.

'Hi,' she welcomed him lightly. 'I didn't think I'd catch you.'

He grinned. 'That's nice.'

'Is it?'

'You were thinking about me—so, yes, it is.'

Kelly smiled shyly, leaning against the wing of the car, feeling the sun flow softly over her skin. 'Well…yes, I was thinking about you but…'

He lifted a finger, pulling a face. 'Don't say it. Don't spoil it.'

Her violet eyes gazed up into the pools of swirling blue and suddenly it didn't matter that she had been going to

make some ridiculous remark just to cover her embarrass-
ment. 'All right.' She nodded, 'I won't.'

'Because I have something very important to say.'

She laughed. 'I'm not sure if that's fair.'

'Oh, it is.'

She could feel his skin burning against hers. His arms
were golden brown, like the limbs of an exotic bronze
sculpture, with fine black hairs running like a waterfall to
curl over his angular wrists. She looked at him in desperation because whatever it was he wanted to say she wasn't
sure if she was ready to hear it.

'You're not on call this weekend?' he asked, and she
took a deep breath.

'No...no, I'm not.'

'And neither am I.' His smile was slow, teasing and in-
credibly seductive. 'I thought I would spend a little time
on the water with Frederico, since we have done no boating
as yet. Perhaps moor in one of the little coves farther
around the coastline. Would you care to join us?'

She couldn't think of anything she would like more. Yet
if she said yes, she would set a precedent for the future.
And did she really want that? After all she'd done to keep
him at a distance.

More to the point, what was happening between them?
Was it just friendship—casual outings—even a little flirtation that really couldn't harm anyone? Or something
deeper, more complex, that had both scared and attracted
her right from the start?

'Are you sure you want me to tag along?' she asked
hesitantly.

'*Almost* a hundred per cent certain,' he replied, crooking
a teasing eyebrow.

'Almost?' She grinned. 'Well, I can't resist the challenge.'

'So now you should sleep,' he advised swiftly, 'and in
the morning I will call for you and we shall enjoy breakfast
on the ocean.'

'Sounds like heaven,' she sighed. 'What time?'

He eased his shoulders into a shrug. 'Nine o'clock. And then we shall have all day.' He paused, a frown slanting its way across his forehead. 'That is, if you have no specific time to return.'

The aquamarine eyes didn't waver, meeting hers with a directness that sent her pulse rocketing as she licked her dry lips. 'No, nothing special,' she managed.

'Good.' His eyes darkened, their deep blue shot with molten silver. 'Then I shall look forward to every moment. Goodnight, *cara*. Sleep well.'

He left her then, walking swiftly away into the surgery, his broad shoulders swaying over slim hips and long, powerful legs, his light linen suit moulding the shape of his body.

Kelly's mind whirled as she drove home. From the first moment she had met Marco, she had known that he was different. So different to any other man she had ever met. That was why she had tried to keep him on the outside of her life. He had no place on the inside and she had done a pretty good job until now.

But suddenly she could hardly wait until she saw him again. No wonder he had been surprised at her swift acceptance today. She had surprised herself, behaving like some love-struck teenager.

Granted, the chemistry was undeniable. But if she had any sense at all, she had better snap out of the spell he had cast. Nothing could come of it except heartache if she took Marco in the least bit seriously.

It could rain, she told herself as she checked her appearance in the mirror, wondering if white shorts and a sun top was tempting fate. There again, she'd piled half her wardrobe into her backpack—one swimsuit, jeans, a sweater, a gauzy top, underclothes, two towels, sunscreen and a dozen other essentials crammed into her bag.

If the weather did change and there was room on the

oat, then there would be no problem. If, on the other hand,
here were no changing facilities and it was one of those
lash but entirely unsuitable craft that sped by at full throt-
le, if she couldn't get to her bag, she'd just have to freeze.

With one last glance at her tall, slender form, thankfully
anned enough now not to worry about burning, she gave
 nod of approval. The soft green sun top was simple, but
retty enough to complement the neat new shorts she had
ust bought from the marina shop. Luckily they had one
ast suitable pair, a small size that normally she would have
ad to hunt down. But they fitted perfectly and felt right
or a day at sea.

That was, if they actually went to sea. The hire boats
vere adequate in the marina, with tiny cabins, and some of
hem were fitted with fishing equipment for the veterans
vho liked to pose out on the cusp of the tidal waters.
Genuine fisherman rarely set off from the marina, choosing
o leave from the harbour on the other side of Charbourne.
So whether it was one of the character boats or something
 little more practical, she had yet to discover.

Was Marco familiar with the channels of the marina? she
wondered. There were sandbanks at low tide but, then, she
hought ruefully as she tucked her freshly washed hair be-
ind her ears and smoothed a dab of perfume behind her
obes, there was always someone about to help with a push
r shove or tow.

In fact, she had been warned herself when she'd hired a
single sailing craft the very first week she had arrived. At
he sailing club, she'd been given a rather unflattering third
degree on her skills and warned that stranded boats were
wo a penny in high season.

But she'd had the sneaking satisfaction of seeing the surprise on the young man's face when she'd sailed back in,
windblown but unharmed and in perfect control of her
rusty little boat. Not that she'd had it all her own way, but
she'd rather have died than admit a wind had sprung up
and she'd had to battle her way around the headland, avert-

ing disaster as another hired boat had skimmed perilously
close across her bow.

It would be somewhat amusing to see how Marco ne
gotiated his way around the marina....

Not fair, she told herself, a teasing gleam in her viole
eyes. It would be no laughing matter if we do get stuck!

Her reflection smiled back at her with just a hint of mis
chief. But then the doorbell rang and her heart leapt out o
her chest, and when she opened it, he was standing there
looking like a Greek god with his sun-kissed dark skin and
thick black hair.

A long-sleeved shirt with the cuffs rolled up fell casually
over his shorts and he slipped his sunglasses an inch dowr
his nose, his bright blue eyes gazing over the rims. They
raked over her with a burning welcome that was far too
flattering not to notice.

'*Buongiorno*, Kelly,' he murmured, his smile tilting so
seductively that whether or not he could handle a boa
seemed utterly irrelevant.

CHAPTER SIX

MARCO held out his hand from the boat moored alongside the jetty. The older man in the cabin turned to grin at Kelly and she smiled back, her hand encased in Marco's as he took her rucksack and smiled.

'Everything but the kitchen sink?' he guessed, lowering the bag to the wooden seat behind him.

'Afraid so.' She nodded, suddenly finding a pair of hands spanning her waist and lifting her easily down into the boat. She couldn't help but gaze into the sunglasses shielding his eyes, wondering what he was thinking. Not that the black lenses made much difference. She didn't know what he was thinking anyway, only that he seemed to be streets ahead of her, an amused light flaring in his blue gaze as the sunglasses had dropped briefly as she had tried to cover her earlier mistake.

Now, as he held her for just a few seconds longer than was necessary, the tension in her muscles felt like an electricity surge and her stomach muscles cramped with a hot tingling awareness.

Being this close to him was bad enough, but as a smile lifted his lips and she saw the curve of his sexy, gorgeous mouth, there was only one thought in her mind. Thank heavens they weren't going to be alone. If she had thought that would happen, then the safest thing to do would have been to turn and run.

In the light of day, involvement with Marco was out of the question. She would be mad to risk being hurt again, just as she had been when her father had disappeared from her life. She simply couldn't go through that torture again. And despite her weak-willed body begging to be seduced

75

by this man, she resolved to exert all her self-control to shore up her pathetically shaky defences.

Just then the engine of the boat revved up. The other man released them from the jetty and got them under way. Reaching out, she was grateful for the opportunity to free herself from Marco's powerful grasp as she stepped backwards and he let her go, his muscled brown arms dropping beside him as he leaned against the cabin.

'Where are Frederico and Isabella?' she asked, uneasily shouting above the noise of the rumbling old engine. Obviously Marco had seen fit to engage one of the hire boat staff for their trip. She was a little disappointed as the boat chugged its way across the water, slowly following the channels. But it was probably the most sensible thing to do. At least they wouldn't end up on a sandbank.

'We're going to meet them.' The sea breeze caught his black hair and lifted it lightly over his forehead. He stood casually, taking the rock of the boat with ease and looking at her with a steady gaze. 'We shall soon be there.'

She saw the little boats bobbing up and down in their wake and wondered if they would pull in at one of the jetties. But they were heading past them, picking up speed as they entered the deeper water. Were they going to leave the marina? Is so, where would they meet Fredrico and Isabella?

She looked back and saw him still smiling, and for a moment she was lost in the sensation of those eyes. Somewhere between fantasy and reality, their relationship defied explanation.

Suddenly the boat slowed down and she stumbled. Marco stepped beside her, his strong fingers spreading out to support the curve of her spine, and something wonderful drifted across with the salt. His own particular brand of musky skin scent and the other cosmetic aroma that was essentially him. Kelly swallowed, leaning against his hard body, all her senses snapping to attention as he held her close.

'I'm mystified,' she confessed, trying to close her mind to the effect he was having on her. 'Where are we?'

'Almost there,' he replied. 'Do you see the little island there?'

Kelly nodded. 'Yes, it's uninhabited, isn't it? I sailed round it when I first came to Charbourne.'

'It's a conservation area, a mile or so in diameter. But it's a beautiful place to drop anchor. Isabella and Frederico are on board, preparing breakfast.'

'On board?' Kelly repeated. 'But I thought *this* was our boat.'

Marco grinned, his hand slipping away from her back now that she had regained her balance. 'Did you think I intended us to spend the day on this boat?'

She smiled uncertainly. 'No, I just assumed you would hire a boat.'

'If I had,' he told her as his eyes filled with amusement, 'it would have been something a little more comfortable than this.'

She laughed. 'So what should I expect? A yacht?'

He narrowed his eyes thoughtfully. 'Well, the *Sandpiper* is certainly closer to that description.'

She had only been joking, but as they rounded the wooded island she saw three or four big boats moored on the clear blue stretch of water.

'Not one of those,' she gasped, her jaw dropping.

He nodded, pointing toward a large white cabin cruiser that made the boat they were standing on seem like a toy. She had sailed by these gleaming, luxurious vessels in her little sailing boat, admiring their elegance as she'd gazed up, never dreaming she would be a guest on one of them.

'There is Frederico.' Marco nodded to a small brown figure clad in red shorts, waving fiercely. 'And Isabella.' A taller figure in shorts and T-shirt emerged from below and went to the ladder hanging from the gleaming white hull. 'They insisted they prepare breakfast before you came aboard and asked me to say nothing so that it would be a surprise.'

She laughed. 'Oh, yes, it is a surprise.'

Their old boat bobbed steadily towards the larger one. The sea was so tranquil there was no problem in transferring to the ladder as Marco's hands once again spanned her waist to help her climb aboard.

The hire boat departed and Frederico grabbed her hand, dragging her along the deck to where Isabella stood under a large white sun canopy. A table was prepared with a lavish meal that Marco had loosely termed breakfast. It was far more than that, of course. Golden sticks of crusty French bread, a selection of cold meats, eggs and cheeses, tossed salads and a bottle of wine stacked in ice.

'This is amazing,' Kelly said, overwhelmed.

'The boat is not mine, alas.' Marco shrugged as he came to stand beside her. 'The *Sandpiper* is Antonio's, a little diversion for Laura, purchased just before they married. Now, are you ready to eat?'

'I'm ravenous,' Kelly admitted as she took her seat next to Frederico, who couldn't stop talking, despite Marco's insistence he eat and not talk.

'To our day on the *Sandpiper*,' Marco said eventually as he lifted his glass, meeting Kelly's eyes over the rim. Their liquid blue brilliance was warm and intimate and her stomach had that butterfly sensation as she met them with the same degree of warmth in her own violet gaze. She had to be crazy, she knew. She simply couldn't help herself. He was drawing her closer without laying a finger on her.

And she had no way of defending herself.

The morning was filled with fun and laughter as they ate their meal and relaxed on deck. Isabella brought long iced drinks from the galley below and Frederico continued to entertain them with his charming mixture of English and Italian.

After they had rested, Isabella took Kelly below to

change. The quarters were surprisingly spacious, with two cabins, one a double, and a little galley that was fitted with every conceivable gadget.

Isabella left Kelly in the double cabin, a mixture of luxurious blue-and-gold upholstered seats and bunks with its own *en suite* shower. Kelly found her bag by the door and changed into her white swimsuit, listening to the hypnotic lapping of the water outside as she folded her clothes and hung them in the small, louvred wardrobe.

Isabella returned in a pink bikini, her long black hair flowing over her shoulders. She gazed curiously at Kelly for a moment. 'You look Italian,' she said at length, her eyes resting on Kelly's flawlessly tanned complexion. 'Not an English rose.'

Kelly laughed. 'No, I'm not fair-skinned,' she said, aware that she was closer to Isabella's colouring than the true English complexion. 'My mother was very dark. I take after her.'

'Where does she live?' Isabella thoughtfully wound her long dark hair on the top of her head as she gazed in the full-length mirror.

'My mother died,' Kelly explained as she ran a brush through her short dark hair and curved the wave behind her ear.

'You were young when this happened?'

'In my twenties. I'd just started training.'

'Frederico was just two when my aunt Sophia died,' Isabella said after a while. She paused, her long dark lashes fanning down on her suntanned cheeks. 'So you must forgive him if he follows you around like a puppy. Do you like children?'

Kelly smiled. 'In Frederico's case, yes. He's a lovely little boy.'

Isabella paused. 'I wish my uncle would marry again. But he has never shown any interest in doing so.'

'Not ever?' Kelly asked curiously.

Isabella turned, a wry smile on her lips. 'Oh, there have

been some women—not many—but he is... How do you
say in English—*stubborn*? He has been living too long
alone and is set in his ways.'

Kelly repressed a smile. Isabella was obviously protective of him and was, no doubt, wondering if there was
anything between Marco and herself. However, although
privately she had to agree that when Marco wanted something he pursued it tirelessly, she didn't want to encourage
Isabella's speculation.

'We'd better go up, hadn't we?' she suggested quickly.
'Or they'll be swimming without us.'

'*Si.*' Isabella shrugged and turned to ascend the narrow
stairs, her dark eyes briefly meeting Kelly's.

When they arrived on deck, Marco was standing with
Frederico, leaning against the rail with his broad back
turned toward them. He had changed into black swimming
trunks which accentuated his powerful, masculine build and
for a few seconds Kelly took in every inch of skin and
bone.

His was a faultless physique, shoulder muscles rippling
with a subdued energy as he stood at ease, talking to his
son. The combination of slim hips and long, powerful legs
would have done credit to an athlete. Even his large, well-
shaped feet and long, straight toes had a sculpted beauty of
their own.

She had thought this morning that he'd looked like a
Greek god as he'd stood on the doorstep of her apartment,
but now, almost naked, he reminded her of a wild, untamed
animal, his dark skin showered in the blackest of silky hair.
Only his back and broad shoulders were exempt, glistening
in the rays of the sun as the muscle moved under his skin
like the body of a lean black panther, poised to spring.

Isabella leapt forward and playfully grabbed Frederico.
Marco murmured something in Italian and obediently they
went to sit in the stern of the boat. When Marco's eyes met
Kelly's, she felt self-conscious as colour rushed into her
cheeks.

His eyes fell slowly—far too slowly—down the length of her swimsuit. Its cut accentuated the long span of her legs and the swell of her breasts above the tiny waist that had a few hours before been encased in his hands.

He seemed to find her fascinating as his liquid blue gaze travelled slowly over her body, unashamedly taking in every inch. And even then he was not finished, but leaned back against the rail to devour her appearance with a sensual expression that deepened her blush.

'You look beautiful, Kelly.'

She came to stand beside him. 'The water looks wonderful. Shall we swim here?'

'You do not like compliments?' he said, lifting a brow.

'You pay them too easily,' she replied smilingly.

'Quite the reverse,' he argued. 'Rarely, in fact. And only when deserved. But in answer to your question…' He nodded to the diving platform behind which Isabella and Frederico were sitting. 'Yes, we shall swim here, off the island. The water is very safe. No strong currents. You are a good swimmer, I think.' He used the remark as an excuse to step back a little and gaze at her body as if determining the answer for himself.

'Reasonable.' She nodded, looking down into the blue waters that were almost transparent and praying they would cool her temperature. Because undoubtedly it was soaring with the attention that Marco was paying her.

'Reasonable?' He chuckled. 'An understatement, I am certain. You are very fit, that is obvious. And you told me that you liked to sail and played squash, a claim supported by your delightfully healthy physique. So, yes, I am sure we will enjoy our swimming today—and don't worry about Frederico. He learnt to swim as a baby on our yacht. He is like a little fish in water.'

Kelly turned to look at him. 'You have a yacht?'

He nodded. 'The *Sophia*, named after my wife.' It was the first time he had really talked about her and Kelly caught the flicker of pain as it flashed momentarily in his eyes. 'Antonio and Laura are using her during their stay in Italy,' he continued, clearing his throat.

'Sophia…a lovely name,' she remarked quietly.

'Indeed,' he agreed softly as tiny lines of sadness bracketed his eyes. 'Sadly Sophia only sailed a few times. She became ill very quickly and could not undertake long voyages.'

'I'm sorry,' Kelly murmured. 'How unfair life can be.'

'I, too, thought so at the time.' He shrugged, his eyes still shadowed, then pulled back his shoulders stiffly. 'But after she died I was grateful she did not suffer. And that she left me with a beautiful son who is the purpose of my life.'

To suffer such a dreadful loss must be indescribable, Kelly thought, admiring his self-contained strength. It had seemed a tragedy when her own mother had died in her forties, but Sophia had barely begun her life and had had everything to live for—a baby son and husband who had obviously adored her. Hard on the heels of this thought came another, a curiosity so strong after what Isabella had said that Kelly simply had to ask.

'Have you never thought of remarrying?'

He shifted his position on the rails, turning his back to lean against them. 'I have thought of it, yes.' He glanced at her with a little grin. 'You are curious about me, Kelly?'

She stiffened. 'Not at all. I just—'

He held up his hand, chuckling softly. 'I am teasing again. And now I am the one who is flattered. You show enough interest to ask. And I like that.'

A hot flood of colour swept up into her cheeks. She hadn't meant to encourage him in that way and yet she was curious, yes. Who wouldn't be? Now she knew a little of the family background, it would be untruthful to claim that she was disinterested. All the same, she didn't want to look too keen. 'I have to admit Isabella mentioned your wife. I suppose what she said stirred my curiosity.'

'And what, exactly, did my niece say?' he asked with a tilting smile.

'Nothing much.' She stopped, going red as she wondered how tactfully she could interpret Isabella's remarks.

'She told you that I do not compromise easily?'

Kelly shrugged. 'No, not exactly. Just that you...you are set in your ways.'

He laughed. 'Yes, this is true. To a young girl I probably appear stubborn.'

'No.' Kelly smiled ruefully. 'Her words were strong-minded.'

He grinned. 'Isabella is not always so tactful.'

'She wasn't intending to be tactful, I'm sure. And to be perfectly honest, though I didn't say so, I have to agree with her.'

He stared at her quizzically. 'Am I to take this as a—?'

'Compliment?' she interrupted, grinning.

'*Si.*' He looked at her with curious blue eyes and she thought that this time she would tease him.

'It depends,' she mused. 'Some women would find strong-mindedness in a man very attractive. Others would not.' She stretched, leaning her back against the railings. 'It's all a question of taste.'

There was a moment of silence and then he threw back his head and laughed. 'You are becoming expert in this little game of ours,' he acknowledged, laughter in his eyes. 'Kelly, when the moment is right and we do not have two noisy young people with us, I shall answer all your questions as truthfully as I can.' He crooked an eyebrow. 'And you will answer mine in the same fashion, no?'

She was about to fluster on that one, but he grinned and she knew he was teasing her again as Frederico ran towards them and grabbed her arm.

'Swim, Kelly, swim!' he begged, and he tugged her toward the stern of the boat and the diving platform.

Isabella was the first to dive into the clear blue water, her pink bikini glowing like a brightly coloured fish under the water. Frederico dived in next, his brown body slipping down into the depths like an eel.

'After you, *cara*,' Marco said to Kelly as he braced himself to follow, allowing her space on the platform.

Kelly stepped forward and in one perfectly executed dive slipped into the cool, delicious sea, momentarily aware of the powerful shape that followed, then thrust up with her to the warm, calm surface.

The rest of the morning was spent in the water and although it was prohibited to land on the island, they used scuba equipment to explore the shallow waters. There was so much to see and discover on the sandy ocean bottom, pretty shells and tiny fish.

Despite the occasional jellyfish and the quick wriggling of the sand eels, the waters contained only friendly species and Frederico collected a wealth of treasures and took them back to the *Sandpiper*.

After lunch, Marco slipped on a bright, multicoloured shirt and consulted the charts for the rest of their trip. Kelly and Isabella showered and smoothed cream into their sandy, sea-washed bodies whilst Frederico took the wheel and, under Marco's expert tuition, steered the boat towards the open sea.

When Marco took over and Isabella went to sunbathe in the bows, Kelly sat with Frederico, examining his treasures under the sun canopy. She wore her long gauzy shirt and floppy hat and relaxed on one of the luxurious pillowed chairs. Frederico sat beside her, wearing a bright shirt like his father's, handing her shells and bits of seaweed that he had collected.

They laughed and giggled, his dark sparkling eyes lighting up when she encouraged him to repeat a word. She tried the Italian version, which had Frederico in hysterics, and Marco glanced back at them, his smile broadening as he witnessed their laughter.

When Frederico took his shells below, Kelly lay back

and slipped on her sunglasses. As she lay there drowsily, she couldn't help but feel she had known these people years instead of months.

Isabella had made an effort to make her feel at home and Frederico was a darling child, bright, well-mannered, and affectionate. He had grown up motherless perhaps, but Marco had not let that influence Frederico's upbringing. He had raised his son to be unspoiled and generous.

What had Sophia been like as a person? she wondered as she lay on the edge of sleep. Did Frederico resemble her? Did he have her bubbling, friendly character? Had she loved Marco very much? Had he loved her deeply? As she thought of them together, she felt a small pang of jealousy. Was Marco still in love with his wife? Is that why he had never remarried?

Even in Laura's wedding photos, Sophia seemed conspicuous by her absence. And Isabella had remarked there had been other women in his life, but none he had chosen to marry. Was Sophia too perfect a memory?

Just then she stirred, her thoughts sucked back from sleep as she sensed a shadow over her. She thought Frederico had returned and opened her eyes with a smile.

'I'm sorry,' Marco murmured softly. 'I woke you.'

'I wasn't asleep.' Embarrassed and wondering how long he had been staring at her, she began to get up.

'Don't move,' he said, stretching out a hand to her shoulder. 'May I join you?'

She looked around, sliding off her sunglasses and hat and letting her glossy dark hair fall behind her ears. 'Where are Isabella and Frederico?'

'In the cabins below, taking an afternoon nap.'

Kelly felt her pulse race. They were alone. 'Have we anchored?'

'Yes. In a little cove. When they are awake we can swim ashore.'

She relaxed back and they lay quietly, then suddenly the muscles in her stomach tensed and she knew it was because he was so close. Close enough to touch and smell. And if she didn't speak soon and break the impossible tension, she might do something she would regret for the rest of her life.

'Frederico's English is coming on,' she said shakily, trying to disguise her nervousness. She had to distract her obsessed attention from the long, tanned body sprawled beside her. But she couldn't seem to drag her eyes away. Her gaze felt glued to the glistening muscled calves that were sprinkled with sexy black hair and which in the water had looked so inviting. And the powerful thighs that must surely be the result of some kind of fitness work-out and would have done justice to a marathon runner.

She daren't even think of the hair-roughened chest and honed muscle that lay unexposed under the colourful shirt. It was only her traitorous mind that kept bringing back the vision of the sexy, powerful body that had splashed and dived beside her in the waters off the island.

But the more she tried to calm her thoughts, the more they were in turbulence. And what was worse, he seemed to sense it. Or was she mistaken that she could feel his arm against hers, much closer than when he had sat down, the tiny hairs grazing her sensitized skin?

'Yes, his English is much better,' he acknowledged in a husky voice. 'But now let's speak of more important matters. What questions, Kelly, may I answer for you?'

As usual, he had caught her off guard. 'I don't really have any—'

'*Please*,' he interrupted firmly, startling her, 'don't disappoint me, *cara*. I *want* to tell you about myself, and I want to know more about you.' He smiled ruefully. 'You are wondering if my wife was beautiful?'

Kelly's jaw fell open. 'How did you know?'

'All women wonder about other women. Is that not so?'

Kelly couldn't dispute that piece of logic. 'Well, yes,' she acknowledged half-heartedly, 'but I suspect men do the same, only they don't admit it.'

Marco laughed, a wonderful, involuntary rumbling sound that echoed up from his chest. 'That is true.' He reached across and enfolded her fingers into his. 'Sophia was indeed beautiful,' he said in a quiet voice. 'She was a wonderful mother and fought hard to battle her leukaemia. We grew up together. Our families were very close and there was always an expectation that one day we would marry. Sophia was not trained for a career. She helped her mother in their large household until we married. Frederico arrived almost immediately. And if she had lived, I am certain we would have had many more children.'

Kelly felt a knife-like pain inside her as she imagined Sophia and Marco together and their beautiful, dark-haired children happily playing around them. She swallowed on the lump in her throat at once, realizing how foolish she was being. How could she be jealous of something that hadn't even happened?

'Do you still think of this young man…Tim?' he asked then.

She blinked as he squeezed her hand, reluctantly coming back from the vision of Sophia and Marco surrounded by their happy brood of beautiful children. No, was the simple answer. She had never felt passion for Tim, certainly nothing like the passion that Marco had felt for Sophia. Nothing even close. More a respect on her part for a man who had been good and kind but to whom she had never been able to give her heart.

'Tim?' she murmured distractedly. 'Sometimes.'

'You shared your love of medicine,' he persisted gently. 'Did you ever consider the possibility of children?'

'With Tim?' she repeated. 'No, at least, I don't recall doing so. We were studying too hard to think about kids—the long-term future. I know Tim wanted to settle down after he'd qualified—but it was something we never really discussed.' She bit down hard on her lip, reluctant to revisit the emotional minefield that she had buried away years ago.

'And so it all ended,' he murmured. 'Do you regret your decision, Kelly?'

She shrugged, not wanting to meet his eyes. To reveal how envious she had been when she'd seen the close relationship he'd shared with Frederico. To think that she might have had a future, a family with Tim, if she'd really tried. But, no, *trying* to fall in love with someone just wouldn't work. She had known it then and she knew it now, more than ever as she had come to know Marco.

'I ask too much perhaps,' he conceded.

She met the dark pools of blue and found his eyes burning into her as if searching for the answers she just could not give. Perhaps didn't even know herself.

He lifted her hand, rubbing his fingers over her knuckles and smoothing the skin of her ring finger. His eyes came up to meet hers and suddenly she forgot about everything, because whatever it was he was doing to her made her mind a numbed blank to reality, to everything but the exquisite sensation of his touch. She could feel his breath on her face and the soft mixture of musk and cologne that was spellbinding her senses.

She knew he was going to kiss her and she knew there was nothing on earth she wanted more. Even if the planet opened up and swallowed her right now, she just didn't care. All she wanted was his mouth on hers as her hand snaked around his strong neck and brought his head down.

CHAPTER SEVEN

THAT was Kelly's last coherent thought before Marco's lips touched hers. As the soft moistness of his mouth closed over hers, she felt a thrill of exhilaration and everything else paled into insignificance.

Tim Baxter, her father, the past and even the future, with all the desire that was banked there for her goals to mate-rialize—she forgot it all in a moment of absolute present, a realisation of pure joy. It was hers, in that kiss. And she knew with certainty that this was how it should be between a man and a woman. No reservations, doubts, uncertainties. And most of all, no courageous attempt to make the kiss what it should be and not what it was.

Fabulous little shudders of excitement travelled up and down her spine as he drew her closer, his hands moving through her hair as his kiss grew deeper. Explosions of bright colour erupted in her brain as her hands explored the hard muscle she had only admired before.

Now she knew what he felt like as he moved against her, trailing kisses over her face, cheeks and neck. And her arms went tightly around him, her body quaking under his gaze.

'*Cara*,' he whispered, and his hands slipped down to the base of her spine and pulled her closer. 'What do you do to me?'

She hadn't a clue. Only that he was doing it to her, too. For all the energy she had expended in trying to stop this from happening, she needn't have bothered, she thought helplessly as his hands moved over her back. His thumbs rubbed against her gauzy shirt and the fragile cloth surren-dered under the heat.

Then his mouth came down again, so that her breasts

pressed hard against his chest and his body melted against hers, the little buds of erotic desire peaking under her swimsuit.

His tongue found hers and tangled with it in exquisite knowledge, so that every second they were linked she felt them moving into place. As if nature itself had designed them for this moment. She wanted him so much her stomach cramped and she slid shaky fingers to the curve of his mouth.

'Marco, we can't,' she protested weakly, and inclined her head toward the stairs. 'Not here…not now…'

He nodded, bringing his lips to her ears, whispering words that she had no hope of understanding. But the sound was so sensual and sexy her stomach clenched again and she felt helpless with longing as she closed her eyes and arched her neck so that he could gain access to her throat.

'Oh, Kelly, I don't want to let you go,' he growled as he brought her to him again, and she knew she had to stop before someone walked up on deck and found them. It was the thought of discovery that gave her strength and she pushed him away, her violet eyes imploring his help. 'Marco, please…'

He stiffened, as though suddenly coming awake. His eyes flicked open to melt over her and he nodded, releasing her slightly. 'Yes, of course,' he muttered, clearing his throat and gently setting her free. It was the first time she had seem him look this way. Not quite in control, uncertain of himself.

She straightened her shirt and slid her feet to the deck. She needed space, air to breathe. The oxygen around them felt too rarefied, as though it had been sucked away by their intensity.

'I…I think I'll swim,' she said, rising to her feet, but he held her arm.

'Kelly?'

'Don't apologize, Marco.'

'I was not about to,' he interrupted, a shadow of the old

amusement flickering over his face. 'I was going to say that I shall join you soon. But first I will wake the young ones.'

She nodded, playing the game, knowing that a swim was just an excuse. They both needed to come to terms with the force of what had just happened. Clearly their desire had overtaken them.

But was this what their relationship was all about?

Beyond the undoubted intensity of their emotions, what did they have in common? She looked into his eyes and he released her and she turned and walked to the diving platform. Peeling off her shirt, she felt his eyes on her and she dived in, never feeling more grateful for the shock of the cold water than now.

For Isabella and Frederico, the change in the weather that evening was a huge disappointment. A squall sprang out of nowhere and Marco was forced to make a dash from the open sea as thunderclouds gathered. The ocean lifted the bow of the boat and dropped it heavily between waves. Though this excitement went some way to consoling Frederico, Kelly saw he was disappointed.

She was certain he suspected nothing of what had gone on earlier that day. But their return home came none too soon for Kelly. An edge of tension played between Marco and herself that was impossible to conceal, and Isabella had been watching them curiously.

Marco steered them into calm water and Frederico joined her in the cabin as she packed her bag. 'This is for you,' he told her, dropping a shell into her hand. He'd washed and polished it and she hugged him gratefully.

'It's beautiful, thank you, Frederico.'

'Papa likes you.' He giggled and hot colour washed up her neck.

'I should hope so.' She tried to dismiss his comment, but without success.

'Do you like him?'

'Of course I like your Papa but—'

'Will you come on the boat again soon?'

She laughed softly. 'Maybe. We'll have to see.'

It seemed to satisfy him and he helped her zip up her bag and struggled with it up the stairs. She followed, wishing that he wasn't so lovable and, above all, that she wasn't giving him false hope for something that just couldn't be.

Marco and Isabella were waiting but there was too much to pile into the little dinghy so Marco called the hire boat on his mobile. Finally they arrived, tired and happily exhausted, at her front door.

'Why don't you all come in for supper?' Kelly offered, but Marco shook his head and grinned.

'I wouldn't inflict that on you. Besides, it's late.'

'I've had a wonderful day,' Kelly murmured.

He leaned forward and kissed her, just a whispering brush on each cheek and the touch of his fingers on her arm. 'Sleep well, *cara*.'

She watched him walk back to his car, his long, powerful legs striding under dark shorts revealing a tantalizing swell of muscle as he closed the door.

Frederico and Isabella waved and then they were gone. Kelly slid her key into the lock and sank into the first chair that presented itself, closing her eyes and wondering if today had been just another extension of her increasingly wanton imagination.

On Sunday Kelly wondered if Marco would phone, but he didn't and without the sound of his voice the day seemed empty. But on Monday they were back to full staff again and queues that were neverending. It was now the first week of August.

'Bedlam,' Joanne said expressively as she handed Kelly a sheaf of notes and unsigned prescriptions. 'And look what I've got for you.'

Kelly grinned. 'Just what I was hoping for.'

'Oh, there's masses more if that doesn't keep you occupied.' Joanne laughed. 'Have a nice weekend? You've got a great tan.'

'Hmm, pretty good.' Kelly buried her face in one of the hospital reports. 'Send my first one if you like, Jo. I'm ready.'

'I hope you are,' the receptionist said, and disappeared.

Kelly breathed a sigh of relief, grateful they were busy enough to counteract small talk. Not that she minded, really. But on this occasion...

Kelly stopped, just, from mindlessly reviewing Saturday over again and looked up to see Hannah James pushing a buggy through the door. She looked tense, Kelly thought as she sat down in the chair and rocked the buggy.

'We called him Patrick.' She smiled as two bright button eyes sparkled back under a cap of blond hair. 'He's six weeks already but it only seems like yesterday when you and Dr Dallori came to the house and rescued us.'

Kelly laughed. 'It was quite a day. How are you feeling?'

'So-so.' Hannah shrugged. 'I'm trying to breast-feed and I feel guilty being here when I've got the midwife calling...' She sighed softly. 'But I just don't seem to be able to feed him very well.'

'In what way?' Kelly frowned.

'I'm in agony. I've used shields and pads and expressed the milk myself but my breasts are a mess. The midwife said I've got rather inverted nipples and that was why it was a problem. But that if I persevered it would probably sort itself out.'

Kelly told her to slip off her blouse and as Hannah removed her bra, she winced. 'Ouch. That looks painful. Why didn't you come to see me before?'

'I just kept hoping it would get better.'

'Well, I'm afraid this won't without help,' Kelly said as she gently examined the swollen, infected breasts. 'You've got mastitis and a nasty infection that we'll have to do something about pretty smartly.'

'With drugs?'

'I'm afraid so.'

Hannah looked miserable. 'So I won't be able to breast-feed?'

'You can't anyway—not until you start healing. And even then, you may have to consider formula if the same problem occurs.'

'Oh, dear,' Hannah sighed, pulling on her blouse.

'Formula feeding isn't the end of the world, you know.'

'But everyone says how important it is to breast-feed.'

'Not at the cost of your health,' Kelly said gently as she typed up a prescription. 'Breast-feeding doesn't suit everyone. Bottle-fed babies develop quite satisfactorily.'

'But I haven't bought bottles or anything,' Hannah protested.

'I'll ask the midwife to visit today and she'll sort you out. Come and see me again in a week, or before that if you're worried. Or would you like me to call?'

Hannah shook her head as she stood up. 'No, I only live a few minutes away, as you know. It's nice to get out. And thank you so much for what you did for us when Patrick was born. It was such a relief for Phillip to offload.'

Kelly smiled. 'Dr Dallori is very approachable, isn't he?'

'Extremely.' Hannah grinned as she turned the buggy around. 'Just how do you manage to keep your mind on your work?'

She didn't—that was the honest answer, Kelly thought dryly as she saw Hannah to the door, clutching her prescription, and said goodbye.

Marco slipped in later. He looked tanned and gorgeous and she completely forgot her resolve to keep her mind on her work. 'Hello,' he whispered as he drew her up and into his arms and kissed her thoroughly, and the last little crumb of her resistance flew out of the window.

'That was…long awaited,' he murmured, holding her close and drawing his fingers through her hair, tucking the glossy wing behind her ear. 'And totally unprofessional.'

'Yes,' she sighed as her stomach flipped. 'It was.'

'Sorry,' he growled softly, kissing her again. 'And I don't have an excuse.'

Kelly shrugged. 'You don't need one.'

He held her face in his hands. 'You look beautiful. Oh, but I forgot. I am not allowed to tell you this.'

She gave him a crooked little smile. 'I can hardly object.'

He gazed into her eyes and heaved a sigh that seemed to come from the bottom of his chest. Then reluctantly he released her and they sat in a civilized manner, though Kelly felt anything but civilized. She wanted his arms around her again and the warmth and strength of his chest against her and the whisper of his breath against her face.

'I rang the police to find out how the case is going against the man who attacked Tania Farlow,' he said as he recovered himself and pushed a hand through his hair. 'They are still trying to compile evidence against him.'

'Trying,' Kelly emphasized dully.

'And then I rang the hospital. They have no plans to discharge her in the immediate future.'

Just then the phone rang and Joanne said her last patient was on the way in.

Marco stood up. 'Perhaps we can make a visit to the hospital after work?'

'Friday?' she suggested, and he nodded then came to stand beside her.

'When shall I see you again—alone?'

All she wanted to do was wrap her arms around him and she knew she couldn't, so she said a little too firmly, 'I'm on call until Thursday.'

'And I'm on duty at the weekend.'

'Which leaves Friday—and the hospital.'

'Perhaps afterwards…?'

She nodded, her heart racing at the expression in his eyes. But then there was a tap at the door and he straightened and moved swiftly towards it. 'Ah, Mrs Frost,' he said warmly, as the tiny woman entered. 'How nice to see you.'

'And you, Dr Dallori. You're still here, then?'

Marco chuckled softly. 'Oh, yes, indeed.'

'If I'd known, I would have booked my appointment with you,' the elderly woman teased. 'No offence to Dr Anders. But you're likely to disappear one day and we shall never see you again.'

A remark which had Kelly wondering if she was crazy to be doing what she was doing. Namely, to consider a relationship with a man who was as impermanent in her life as yesterday's fresh bread. Common sense seemed to have deserted her in more ways than one. Her relationship with Marco could only ever be an illusion and there was no way in the world that it could ever be more.

They found Tania sitting in a chair beside her bed when they arrived on Friday. She wore her dressing-gown and Sister explained that was because she had just come back from X-Ray. Marco went in search of chairs and Kelly arranged the flowers she'd bought in a vase.

'They're lovely, thanks,' Tania said quietly.

'How are you?' Kelly asked, perching on the bed.

Tania shrugged. 'All right.'

'Are the ribs painful?'

'A bit. They thought one had splintered when I first came in. They're still checking my lung but it seems OK. Sister explained it all, something about my chest moving in the wrong direction when I breathe.'

Kelly sat down on one of the chairs that Marco brought. 'Flail chest, I think you mean. Rib fractures sometimes cause the chest wall to move in the opposite direction to normal.'

Tania pushed back her long fair hair. 'I've been having physio. They make me hold my side as I breathe, which isn't that easy with this thing on my arm.' She raised the cast hidden under her sleeve. 'They've put metal pins into the wrist bone and a frame round it to keep it all in place. It's like a lead weight on my arm.'

'Immobilization is the only way they can make certain you heal,' Marco explained. 'Have you had any more thoughts on what you're going to do when you leave here?'

Tears threatened but Tania held them back. 'There's no way I can stay in Charbourne. I told you why.'

'Have you spoken to the police again?' Kelly asked.

Tania shook her head firmly. 'No. I don't want to see them.'

'Because you don't want to press charges?'

'Because I *can't*,' Tania sobbed, a tear escaping.

'Would it make any difference,' Marco said quietly, 'if you knew this man was going to prison?'

Tania frowned. 'Why do you say that?'

'If you were to tell them who did this to you, there would be even more evidence to put this man behind bars.'

'Think about it,' Kelly said as Tania lapsed into silence, and after a few moments, they got up to leave. Kelly was preoccupied as they walked down the hospital corridor and out to Marco's car.

'I don't know that we helped very much,' she sighed as they climbed in.

'It would help if she would speak to a counsellor, but Sister said she is still refusing to see anyone, except her friend Lyn.'

'I suppose that's something,' Kelly murmured as he switched on the engine and drove out of the car park.

'And now?' His voice made her turn and she met his eyes. 'Remember, it's Friday,' he said, and some of the tension in his face disappeared.

She remembered. She had been thinking about this moment all week. Yet she felt preoccupied after their visit to the hospital.

'Come home with me,' he said softly. 'Isabella and her friend have taken Frederico to the sports club. They will not be back until nine.'

* * *

It was half past seven when they reached his apartment. A scorching sun had just dipped beyond the pool and a sultry pink wash glowed in its wake. The vapour trail of a jet curved a huge white eyelash over a turquoise backdrop and the aroma of barbeques filled the air as Kelly leaned her back against the warm stone of the garden wall.

Marco brought long iced lemonade drinks to the patio table and they sat until the sun completely disappeared, sipping and talking, arms touching and the frisson of tension between them too strong to be able to concentrate on anything but incidentals.

'It's beautiful here,' she said as they looked out over the pool water where the sparkles of light danced like jewels.

'It is,' he agreed, his eyes feasting on her, and she smiled self-consciously.

'But I miss the noise—the activity of Frederico and Isabella. The place seems almost too quiet.'

'For the moment, that seems appropriate.'

She swallowed. 'Marco, I don't know what I'm doing here.'

'Then let me remind you,' he said in a husky, sexy voice that shattered the remnants of her composure. 'You have come at my request, so that for a short while we can be alone. Nothing has to happen, Kelly, if that is what you are frightened of. Though at this moment I want nothing more than to hold you close, to touch you, to feel you against me. Do you want that, Kelly?'

How could she say that she didn't? She'd been dreaming of it, imagining it, wanting it so much that if Friday hadn't come she could willingly have died. And now all she could do was think of all the reasons why it was such a bad idea. Not that her body had the slightest inclination to take any notice of her mind. She was trembling and her legs had become immobile and her heart was crazily bouncing inside her chest.

She nodded, gripping her empty glass. 'Yes,' she murmured, and he reached out, prising her fingers from the glass and wrapping them into his own as he stood up and led her into the apartment.

It was cool and smelt of something heavenly, probably the lilies that were arranged so perfectly in a tall vase on the marble tiles. She inhaled, already intoxicated as he led her to the big sofa. She sank down beside him and he lifted her chin.

'Don't be frightened,' he said, and she gazed into the deep blue eyes that held her spellbound. He kissed her slowly, meltingly, moving her against him so that she fitted as though she had been made for his embrace. Her fingers slid up to the black hair that spilled over his shirt collar and down the strong column of his neck. Neither of them had changed from their working clothes, but it didn't seem to matter as his hands moved over her body, threading softly against her bare skin.

His fingers touched the lacy edge of her bra and carefully moved its restriction. She gave a low moan as his palm cupped the heavy fullness of her breast and teased her with exquisite motion. His breath came raggedly and deeply and she wondered if he was about to stop, or if he could stop, and did it matter anyway?

If he wanted to take her to bed, she wouldn't be capable of resisting. I want you so much, she yearned silently as his mouth claimed her lips and neck and trickled down to her breast as she felt herself falling, hurtling, spinning like a star in some far-off galaxy.

'Kelly,' he whispered, his mouth hot and burning over hers, 'I want you. You know that, don't you?'

She knew it and kissed him back to offer her proof. Her tongue snaked wantonly out to claim the sweetness of his, like a drug, locked together in a desire that was terrifying. She was on a course that she couldn't alter, not now and not ever perhaps. Nothing sane or real about it.

A fantasy, a dream, but she was dreaming it. And if he wanted her as much as she wanted him, she had no way to stop what was about to happen.

And if he'd taken her then to the bedroom, it would have seemed as natural as the breath she was breathing. She craved him so much that she could barely lift her heavy lids and it was all she could do to take air. Their bodies were fused like lovers' and, but for their clothing, the act that was destined to happen between them seemed imminent. Inescapable. A fact of her crazy life and the desire that had her balancing mindlessly on a precipice that led to—where?

Then suddenly, in a moment, it all changed. His mouth came away and he drew her to him, holding her so tightly that she couldn't move. And here they remained, her heartbeat like a drum in her ears, her body pooling with heat. And his heart pounding against her breast as her body shook in his arms.

Neither of them spoke and yet she craved some audible sound, something that would right her topsy-turvy world. But then she felt him shudder and loosen his grip and slowly he peeled her away, his eyes meeting hers with a grim determination that acted like cold water on her desire-crazed senses.

'Wh-what's the matter?' she asked feebly, self-conscious about her dishevelled appearance. Her shaky fingers came up to dither over her clothes and she blushed scarlet as she rearranged her underwear and blouse.

'Nothing is the matter,' he said stonily as he watched her, his face a mask that she had never seen before. 'I am entirely to blame.'

'For what?' She didn't understand what was happening.

'For making this seem…' He searched for the word, his blue eyes steeling with a dark, intense frustration. 'Trivial.'

Trivial? Lying here in his arms had been anything but trivial to her. What they were doing had obsessed her for hours—days—even weeks. Not that she could tell him that. Of course she couldn't.

How could she put into words her decision, that an affair was inevitable? That in her mind she had posed the question and had answered with an affirmative. A relationship for however long or short a time. The little voice inside her head had shouted so loudly she couldn't ignore it. And here she was—as she had known that day on the boat she would be.

For better or worse. He hadn't forced her. She was here of her own volition. And nothing about that choice had been trivial.

'I...I don't understand,' she said helplessly, her body still shaking.

'*Cara*...what have I done?' Marco reached out and took her hands, his eyes filled with an expression that cut to her soul. 'I wanted you so much.'

Wanted? Past tense? Oh, God, she thought in abject humiliation, and her cheeks burned afresh. But before Kelly could speak, he lowered his head and brought her hand up to his mouth. He kissed her fingers and something heavy and wanton beat inside her as she gazed down at his beautiful thick black hair. She still wanted him. Even if he didn't want her. Even if he was going to make some polite, charming excuse—and then just disappear out of her life.... She still craved him.

'Kelly, how can I have let my feelings get out of hand?' He brought his gaze up slowly. 'To expect us to make love—to reach each other in the most important of ways—before my son comes home.' He gave a snort of contempt. 'What happened to me? I saw you in the garden, with the sun streaming through your hair, your beautiful eyes ablaze with the reflection of nature, your body so feminine and warm...'

She stared at him, confused and bewildered. 'Marco, what are you trying to tell me?'

He heaved a ragged sigh. 'Kelly, I said once I want to know all about you. I want to see inside your mind. To know what drives you and what you want from life. Yet tonight I am prepared to make love to you according to the dictates of a clock! My behaviour is inexcusable.'

Her eyes slewed incredulously over his face. 'Did we have any choice?'

'*Si.*' He nodded gravely. '*I* had a choice. I could have taken you to dinner—bought you flowers—made this evening as special as it should be. But what did I do? I lost control and could not see beyond my physical desire.' He looked at her with hooded, heavy eyes. 'And afterwards, *cara*, what would you have thought of me?'

She looked at him in desperation. 'I...I don't know, Marco. You're asking the impossible. You didn't drag me here. I came willingly. We both knew what was going to happen.'

'You are talking,' he said gruffly, 'of sex.' He drew slightly away, his jaw tightening. For a long while he looked at her, then slowly he pulled her towards him and held her gently against his chest, his hands tenderly cupping her as though she were fragile china.

'I want much more than sex, Kelly,' he rasped, and her breath caught fiercely in her throat as somewhere in her muddled brain she realized what he was saying. 'I want you. The real Kelly. We have found something very special. I knew from the first moment I saw you. And tonight we could have thrown it away.' Marco heaved a sigh and tilted her chin up to gaze into her eyes. 'We must begin again. And this time, little one, we must speak the truth.'

'Come,' he said gently, and rose and grasped her hand and drew her into his arms. 'Forgive this impatient man. I want to share so much with you.' He kissed her, a featherlight touch that drifted across her lips like a whispering breeze.

Kelly was too confused to reply. His touch sent traces of fire along her spine and she only knew that he wasn't saying what she had thought he had meant. That he wanted her—but not in the way she had been prepared to settle for. When she got over the shock this all might dawn on her, of course.

If she got over the shock...

'Let me take you to dinner,' he said, curving his hands over hers. 'You remember, I asked once before and somehow you eluded me.' He smiled a gorgeous smile. 'Don't look at me like that, *cara*,' he chided softly. 'We started— how do you say, on the wrong foot? And I only realized tonight, fool that I am.'

She laid her hands on his shoulders, her trembling fingertips against his neck. 'I'm still not certain what's happening,' she said with a shaky little sigh. 'Or what you want of me.'

'Wish for a tomorrow,' he said, one black brow lifting sagely. 'If we had hurtled on without thought, there would have been none.' He lifted her chin. 'A brief encounter would not have endeared you to me. You are not the type for such a thing, Kelly. That much I know about you.'

'Then you know more than I do,' she admitted, wondering if she had been in some kind of trance and was only now coming out of it. 'I had no expectations, Marco. None that I would have expected you to meet.'

'A one-night stand, as they say,' he said with another sigh. 'And though we may have extended it to two or perhaps three, grabbing moments when we could, what would that say about our relationship?'

She moistened her lips with her tongue. 'Relationship?'

'Yes, the one we are about to form.'

'But that's impossible,' she said with a hoarse little laugh. 'You must know that. We come from different worlds…families…countries.'

'Which makes a relationship impossible?' he questioned with wide blue eyes. 'No, *cara*. You are wrong.'

She gazed at him and wished for all the world she believed him. Those beautiful eyes, and the expression in them was sincere. But he was fooling himself if he thought for one minute they stood a chance. They didn't. Even if he didn't know it, she did.

Marco trailed a finger across her lips. 'Trust me,' he whispered as his mouth teased the soft skin of her cheek with impossible delicacy. Then, just as his lips touched hers, they heard the sound of voices outside.

Kelly pushed away, pressing down her blouse and skirt, feeling as though she had taken a leap from one roller-coaster to another, just as Frederico's little face appeared at the big picture window.

CHAPTER EIGHT

THANK heaven, Kelly thought, for a weekend where she knew Marco was absolutely forbidden to her. If he hadn't been on call, she might have done something impulsive, like pestering him on the phone for absolutely no reason at all.

She tormented herself with a thousand silly scenarios and exhausted herself in the gym and playing squash and felt utterly wrecked by Sunday night. But at least she slept and didn't toss over the same old questions that she'd worn out during the day. Like, was he serious about getting to know her better? And, most of all, why?

They were poles apart, geographically. He had a family, a practice, a way of life that he had carved out for himself since his wife's death.

How could she possibly hope to fit into a life already full to the brim? And yet he had told her he wanted to know the real Kelly Anders. That little gem was the one thing she hadn't been prepared for. Even she hadn't allowed the real Kelly Anders to see the light of day. Not for years. Probably since her dad had disappeared and the little girl had grown into a woman overnight.

When she arrived at work on Monday, an avalanche of weekend woes straggled from the desk. All morning, the casualties came thick and fast.

After the tummy bugs and summer colds there was Hannah James, and this time she was alone, looking brighter and more relaxed.

'Well, I've done it,' she sighed as she removed her blouse and bra. 'Patrick seems settled on formula but my breasts are still tender.'

Kelly noted the infection had begun to heal, but not rapidly. 'You're still a bit suspect here and there.'

'I know. But do I need any more antibiotics? I'd rather not if I can avoid it.'

Kelly nodded. 'OK. I think we've caught the worst of it.'

'There's one more thing,' Hannah said as she buttoned her blouse and looked up. 'This isn't a medical issue, but I need a little advice. I know how worried Phil was about me having the baby…so I put off talking to him…' She stopped and sat back with a sigh. 'You see, my family is Jewish and Phil's Roman Catholic. We agreed he would bring Patrick up in his faith as I wasn't practising mine. But now, well, I have this strong feeling—it's difficult to explain—I wish I'd had Patrick circumcised.'

Kelly paused. 'That's a difficult one, Hannah. And I'm not a marriage counsellor.'

'Yes, but as a woman, would you sacrifice an important value for your marriage?'

'I'm not married,' Kelly said thoughtfully. 'But if I was…well, I think I would have to feel strongly about the issue.' She paused. 'Is circumcision important to you?'

'The strange thing is, I didn't think it was. My parents rarely took me to the synagogue, but in marrying a Christian I renounced part of my identity. I married for love and I wouldn't change a day of it. But it seems I still have an internal dialogue going on about my own core values.'

'I wish I could help,' Kelly sighed softly. 'Can you talk to Phillip?'

She shrugged. 'He's had a lot to deal with.'

'Try.' Kelly smiled. 'You won't know until you do.'

Words that could have equally applied to her own circumstances, Kelly reflected as she sat alone afterwards. Hannah had expressed it so clearly—the internal dialogue of childhood continuing into adult life. And with all the will in the world to grow up and away from it, sometimes human beings carried the emotional baggage for ever.

It was a thought that had occurred to her lately more than it had ever done before, when she thought of her father. For some reason he'd chosen to make a life elsewhere. He'd deserted his wife and two daughters and even when Meg and she had spoken to him after their mother's death, he'd seemed like a stranger.

Try as she may to come to terms with the fact, Kelly knew that the past had shaped her present and her dad's rejection had followed her into her relationship with Tim. Not that Tim would have betrayed her. He had been far too good a man for that. Intellectually she had believed in him. But emotionally she had still been that fourteen-year-old, waiting for the father to come home who never did.

Hannah's visit preyed on her mind all day. And it wasn't until she was about to leave that she wondered if Marco was still in the building. He was, she discovered, in his room, surfacing from the paper mountain that threatened to spill over his desk.

He looked up when she entered and she closed the door and leaned against it, meeting his eyes and feeling the bleak emptiness that had engulfed her since Hannah's visit slowly seep away.

He rose and came towards her and they needed no words as he took her in his arms and kissed her. A long, enduring kiss that made a mockery of all her doubts. If she had been thinking about her father before, Marco erased every thought in a matter of seconds.

'Tough day,' he murmured against her hair as his own special scent melted into the air that she breathed and burned through her body.

'I missed you.'

He tilted her chin. 'Say it again, *cara*.'

'I missed you.'

He looked into her eyes. 'It was worth the wait.'

She felt her heart beating under his. 'I didn't realize you were—waiting.'

He smiled, running a finger down her cheek. 'I have been

waiting since the moment I last saw you. All through the weekend and today. Telling myself to be patient, to wait until you were ready…'

'Until I was ready?'

'You may have had second thoughts,' he posed with a questioning frown, his blue eyes drowning her in liquid silk. 'It was quite possible.'

Possible, she thought, but in no way probable. Not a chance. Not now. All she wanted was his arms around her like this as he cupped his fingers along her jaw and trickled his thumb to the curve of her neck and down to the well of her throat.

Kelly wanted his fingers to continue their path and never stop, and she wanted to touch him, too, to know how it felt to hold him, to run her fingers over his body in a way that she had never believed she could want so much.

Try, though, she may, she couldn't do with this man what she had done with Tim. He was, as Isabella had so succinctly pointed out, a man who knew his own mind. And though she'd tried, at first, to sideline him, he'd broken through all her defences. There was no way she could phase him out of her mind, because he was already there. Occupying her thoughts with predatory ease, Marco had simply walked into her head and refused to leave.

'I want to spend time with you…soon,' she murmured as the last vestiges of pride fell around her feet. Other than give way to the urge to beg him to make love to her on the spot, it was about the most civilized answer she could give.

'*Dove ti piacerebbe andare?*' His voice dropped an octave as he relapsed into his sensual native tongue, and she groaned softly.

'That sounds beautiful, even if I don't know what it means.'

He grinned, clicking his tongue. 'Where would you like to go, *cara*?'

There was, of course, only one truthful answer, but she

couldn't give it. There was nothing on earth that she would rather do than curl up in his arms and forget the world existed. Instead she murmured, 'Somewhere romantic.'

'Of course,' he murmured seductively. 'And after-wards…since Frederico and Isabella are away for the week-end…the night will be ours.' And there it was, the promise that she could only have dreamed of before today…

He gazed into her eyes with a passionate, almost animal hunger. And as if committing the moment to memory, he kissed her deeply before finally letting her go.

Whatever it was that she'd seen in his expression, it had touched somewhere exquisitely pleasurable inside her. That no one crossed her path on the way to her room was a miracle, and as she sat at her desk her heart pounded heavily.

Four days. They would seem like four years.

It was Liam who first fell victim to the flu. He struggled until late that afternoon, but at four Jamie sent him home.

'He looked shattered,' Jamie said as Kelly met him in the office as they shared out the rest of Liam's patients. 'I hope to goodness we haven't got a summer bug doing the rounds. I had two in today on the borderline.'

'Me, too,' Kelly admitted, casting her mind back to the little girl of nine with a headache and sickness. Her mother had said she felt ill today and Kelly had suspected a virus. And when Joanne added that she had a list that would stretch to seven o'clock, their fears were confirmed.

It was eight before Kelly got home that night and it started all over again at eight the next morning. Sore throats, sickness and headaches and a variation on a theme that would have done justice to a winter virus. Whatever it was, Kelly reflected as she trawled through a desperate morning, it was running rife.

By Thursday, half of Reception had succumbed and they were managing on a wing and a prayer. Liam was off sick still and Jamie went down next, looking as wretched as Kelly had ever seen him.

They had to get in a locum and by Friday the waiting room sounded like a battlefield. Coughing and wheezing, a choir of dishevelled sniffers and blowers attended her surgery one by one.

She could do very little, of course. The virus was aggressive and, though only one half to one hundredth the size of the smallest bacteria, it spread like ink on blotting paper and engulfed even the potently healthy.

It didn't discriminate. She had marathon runners and eighty-year-olds falling like flies, and with many all she could do was alleviate the symptoms and trust the body's immune defences to bring a cure.

She had worked late every night and taken two on-call duties that hadn't been hers. And by three o'clock she'd had no lunch, not that she felt like it.

She drank lots, as she had advised all her patients to do. And she gave in at five to a coffee and muffin that Michelle brought her.

'Eat…' Michelle grinned '…before you drop.'

Kelly smiled and lifted her arms and stretched noisily. 'I can't resist that. It looks gorgeous.'

'I'm holding off the rest of your list for ten minutes. You didn't get a lunch-break. And, I'm sorry to say, we've still got them trailing in. This bug's a nightmare.'

'How are you fixed on the desk?' Kelly asked, nibbling the cake and gulping coffee.

'Joanne's gone home. Achy legs, sickness and tummy upset. Maggie's still on her feet and Julia is, too. Otherwise it's just yours truly.'

'Can you cope?'

'Well, if I can't, you'll soon know.' Michelle grinned again. 'They'll all be storming your room, screaming for attention.'

'OK.' Kelly nodded, pushing away her plate. 'I'm done. And thanks, Michelle. Oh, how's the locum doing?'

Michelle rolled her eyes. 'He's no idea where anyone lives, of course. So Dr Dallori introduced him to the computer map and printed directions.'

The thought of the following evening flickered across her mind as Michelle left and the door clicked behind her. There was no way she was going to be able to leave early tonight. The pipe dream of a hairdo and manicure was totally blown. And as for something to wear, well, she might just catch the little boutique in the town centre.

Her next patient was a young man who looked quite ill, with a cough that racked his chest. 'It's probably flu,' he wheezed. 'They're dropping like ninepins at work.'

She sympathized and examined him and found no secondary infection and told him the same thing as she had told countless others. 'Go to bed. Drink plenty of fluids, warm ones in your case to soothe your throat, take paracetamol and don't eat if you don't feel like it. It will pass, be patient.'

She saw three more variations on the same theme, then prayed she could escape. But it was six by the time she flew into the boutique. She tried on three dresses and bought the last—a slim-fitting blue silk creation to die for.

Just as she was leaving, her mobile went and Michelle told her there was one patient the locum couldn't manage. She fought off the urge to collapse and saw the poor man, swept off his feet by the same bug. And the town-centre clock chimed eight when she finally drove home.

It was five next morning when she woke, fully dressed, on the sofa. She groped her way to the bathroom and two hours later she had her head over the loo, wishing the earth would open up and swallow her.

'I'll never make it,' Kelly shuddered into the telephone. 'I'm so sorry.'

'I'll come over.'

'No. I'll crawl back to bed and sleep it off.'

'Leave the door open,' he insisted. 'I'll be there.'

'But I'll end up giving it to you. And you're the only one left on your feet.'

Marco muttered something inaudible and the line went dead. She hobbled to the front door and slid the latch. The nausea had abated, but she felt on fire and her stomach protested as she passed the kitchen.

The bed was a mess and she couldn't find the strength to make it so she crawled back in and covered herself with the sheets and lay there.

He arrived quietly, but she heard the latch go. Her eyes flickered open and she saw his tall figure weave in and settle on the bed, his hand going straight to her forehead. 'How long have you been like this?' he asked, scowling over a thermometer.

'Middle of the night, I think.'

He smoothed back her damp hair. 'You're wet through. I'm going to sponge you down and lower that temperature.'

Under normal circumstances she would have welcomed the attention, but the thought of him seeing her like this, a bundle of goose-bumped flesh under a crumpled T-shirt, was terrifying.

'I'll be all right,' she protested, but he walked away and there was nothing she could do except try to swallow on the dry sticks lodged like stakes in her throat. He came back with a bowl and sponge and wrapped her in his arms and lifted her onto the futon, as though she were no weight at all. In a fog of nausea she curled there as he draped a cover across her, then turned his attention to the bed.

She wasn't too ill to watch his easy, economic movements and he must have found the fresh linen because she smelt the fabric softener as the fresh sheets fluttered down. When the pillows were plumped and the bed was made, he scooped up the pile of laundry and disappeared. Seconds later he was on his knees beside her, sponging her face and her lips with a gentle concern that almost brought tears to her eyes. And probably would have if she'd had the energy to weep.

'Arms up, little one,' he said as he lifted each side of her T-shirt, deaf to her feeble protest as he dragged the soggy fabric over her head. What might have quite easily seemed an indignity he somehow made like a work of art, as his eyes for one brief moment slid appreciatively down over the damp, full swell of her breasts. The moment was swift, thank heavens, even as they dragged lower to the flat slope of her stomach made barely decent by an edge of white panties.

Then, apparently recovered, he began to sponge her, his touch so light and beautiful that they could have been making love if she wasn't so out of it.

Despite the fever, or maybe because of it, she submitted, his dark eyes roving over her nakedness, not with detachment but with a tight control that made her wonder what he was thinking. He worked the sponge over her breasts, softly curving over her nipples as they peaked involuntarily. His gaze slid up and she knew that if she hadn't been shaking like leaf, with just about every inch of skin on fire, she would have tried to pull up the cover and cut short the sweet torment.

But the thought flickered out of focus as he continued, bathing her arms, wrists and hands and in between her burning fingers with cool water that felt like heaven. He healed her inside even as she watched him, his handsome face intent on his ministrations, his white shirtsleeves rolled up and the top button undone, a twist of fine black hair nudging over the cotton.

Then his eyes slid down to her white panties and she almost threw up.

'No...no more,' she begged, her throat tightening, and tenderness replaced the desire that had burned briefly in his eyes. 'Th-there's fresh nightwear in the drawer—over there,' she gabbled, and a smile thudded his lips as he lifted the towel and dabbed her gently.

Her heart thudded as he rose, the absence of his touch more pain than pleasure. Then a wave of nausea came and she curled her legs to her stomach, attempting to ease the discomfort.

'This, *cara*?' he asked as he sat on the futon and shook out a sleeveless cotton nightie.

She nodded and he helped her to sit up, threading her fingers through the sleeves and stroking the damp hair from her face. She flopped back, helpless and panting, and tears sprang to her eyes.

'Sorry,' she sniffed. 'I'm useless.'

'So I have the advantage—at last,' he teased, and she managed a smile.

'Marco…you don't have to be here.'

'No,' he agreed calmly, 'I don't.'

'What about Frederico?'

'He's with Isabella, remember? Staying with Isabella's friend's parents for the weekend.'

'I forgot,' she sighed shakily. 'This was our weekend, wasn't it?'

'There will be more,' he assured her, curling her into his chest and lifting her back into bed. He dropped a kiss on her burning cheek and minutes later she felt herself drifting—or falling, she couldn't decide which—as sleep blissfully took all the sickness away.

Kelly woke in darkness with a raging headache.

A speck of light under the door grew into a beam and she must have been delirious because she knew Marco was beside her, mopping her down and whispering words of comfort. His face was a blur but she clung to his strength as her stomach lurched with violent waves and subsided to leave her drained and empty.

'Drink this,' she heard at some point in the night, and she tried. Her will to drink was there as her lips sucked from the glass, but her stomach still refused nourishment. It all came up minutes later and he mopped her down and patiently dried her out and she drifted back into a fog of merciful sleep.

In the morning, she opened her eyes to see him, stretched out on the futon, his head on a bundle of pillows, his eyes with their crescent moons of thick black lashes still on his high-boned cheeks. He wore blue shorts and a sweatshirt and on the table was the bowl and sponge and beneath a whole new pile of laundry.

He'd changed her again because she was in a different nightie and the sheets were white, not pink. He lay there in a shaft of beautiful sunlight and his dark hair flopped over his forehead, one bronzed arm fallen to the floor, his broad chest rising steadily.

She wanted to watch more, to feast her eyes, and she thought for a moment she felt better. But a grey nausea swept in and she knew the bug wasn't done with her. She prayed for sleep and closed her eyes and wondered when, if ever, she would feel right again.

Her dreams were desperate and wretched. Dad was going away again and she was waiting, watching from her bedroom window, and Mum and Meg were crying. It was a familiar dream, but this time Dad returned, but he was with someone else. A little girl, with dark hair and big, sad violet eyes. And though he wanted to come back into the house, she wouldn't let him, tugging his hand and leading him into the distance. Kelly knew even in the dream she was shouting, trying to make them stop, to tell them the door was open…

'*Mi amore*…' The words billowed softly into her nightmare and kindly dispelled it.

She opened her eyes, with lids that felt as heavy as rocks.

'I'm here,' he murmured and squeezed her hand. 'You're quite safe, Kelly.'

'I w-was dreaming.'

'I know. But you're awake now.' Marco lifted her head and pressed her lips to a glass. 'Drink, little one. This time it will stay down.'

Nervously she sipped and waited. The water seemed to

settle and he told her to drink more, so she did and, thank heaven, it stayed down.

'That's better.' He smiled and sat on the bed and she felt the indentation of his weight under her. Slowly she focused her eyes.

'How long have I—?'

'Two days,' he told her, taking her hands between his own and stroking them with the smooth pads of his thumbs. 'It's Monday—and you are looking beautiful again.'

She smiled at this. 'Liar.'

'Do you think you could eat?' He propped her up on the pillows, cupping her shoulders between his hands.

'Not yet. Soon, though.' She raised her arm to look at her watch. Even that small movement cost her dearly and her head spun like a top. 'Monday…the surgery…it's seven already.'

'Don't concern yourself, *cara*. All is arranged. I phoned Liam last night. He's back this morning. And so is Jamie. And I shall take your list for those who will see me, or they will rebook for you.'

She realized he was in his suit trousers and a clean white shirt that was almost as dazzling as the smile he bathed her in. He'd shaved and showered and smelt so wonderful that even the breeze from the sea flowing in from the open window couldn't compete. 'Have you been here all weekend?' she asked incredulously.

'Yes—and although I have to leave you this morning, I shall return at lunchtime. We'll eat then, OK?'

She nodded, the muscles in her neck cramping with even that small effort. 'I'll get up—'

'No,' he told her, pressing her back as she struggled to lift her head. 'No way. You need to sleep. To regain your strength. Tonight perhaps, for a short while, when I am with you.'

'But Frederico and Isabella…'

'I have spoken with them and they are staying away a

few more days. So I have nothing to do but help you recover.'

She laughed shakily. 'Yes, Doctor.'

'Your mobile is here beside you. And there's water and a toothbrush and toothpaste. When you've slept, you can brush up a little, but I shall be back at one.'

Kelly felt her eyes growing heavy again. He was right, damn it, she couldn't fight the exhaustion. His fingers trailed over her hair and, try as she may to stay awake, her lids closed like lead weights.

But this time she slept peacefully and didn't even hear Marco leave. She had no dreams that woke her in a fright with her heart pumping like a generator. Instead, she dozed lightly, waking at intervals to the sound of the marina coming to life through the open window.

The white muslin curtain lifted on the breeze and the room was dappled with morning sunlight. Little by little, small memories returned. His strong arms around her in the dark, hot night, comforting and tender as the fire had burned up her body like an incinerator. Water sponged over her head and lips and body, cooling her as she'd fought for air in what had seemed like her own private hell. His voice, whispering in her ear, flowing over her burning body like a cool, revitalizing breeze. And his eyes this morning as she'd raised her lids, like the promise of spring on a dark winter's night.

CHAPTER NINE

IT WAS a long haul. Much longer than Kelly had expected. She'd lost weight, too, which was a bind because clothes didn't fit and she thought longingly of the new dress hidden in her wardrobe that she'd never worn for their night of romance.

Marco was still at her side every spare moment he got, forcing her to eat when she would rather not have. But he made soups and scrambled eggs and looked mortified when she could only manage a few spoonfuls. So she persisted, her taste buds protesting with every swallow, but she was grateful and didn't want to disappoint him.

Isabella and Frederico came home on Wednesday and phoned her in the evening just as Marco arrived. 'We played crazy golf,' Frederico told her exuberantly. 'Can we come to visit you?'

'Soon,' she promised.

'Can I phone tomorrow?'

'That would be nice.'

'He said he missed you and wanted to ring the moment he got in the door,' Marco told her as she put the phone down and watched him settle a box full of groceries on the coffee-table.

'I missed him. Shouldn't you be at home? I really can manage now, Marco.'

He sat beside her on the sofa, slewing one long arm over the cushions behind her. 'They've had a long day. I ate supper with them and told them not to wait up. Now, how are you feeling?'

'On top of the world,' she lied easily.

'I'd believe you if you weren't so pale.' He trickled a

118

hand down her cheek. He looked tired but she knew he would never admit it. Her list had been endless for this week and though some of her patients had rebooked, she knew he had absorbed the others. But he had shrugged it off and brought her flowers and restocked her fridge and force-fed her whenever he'd had the chance.

He'd been wonderful and she didn't know why. And now with Frederico saying he'd missed her, it was really too much.

'*Cara*, what is wrong?' Marco frowned as she stiffened away from his touch. It made it worse when he was so caring. 'Are you feeling sick again?'

'No. I'm fine. Really.'

'Kelly, something is wrong.'

She was terrified she was going to burst into tears and she didn't know why. 'It's just that you're all so nice to me,' she mumbled into his chest.

He laughed shortly. 'And that upsets you?'

'No, of course it doesn't. But…'

'What?'

For a long time he stared at her, waiting for her response, but what could she say? The urge to trust him was overwhelming. She'd been prepared to go to bed with him before she'd been ill, so why was she reacting like this?

A lot had happened since then, a little voice inside her head bit back. You're not playing games or dealing in fantasies any more. This man is for real. He has no intention of allowing you to keep him at a distance. Because that was your plan, Kelly Anders, wasn't it?

She felt a blush steal into her face at the thought. She'd divided her physical needs and her emotional ones in two, making little compartments of her life just as she always had since a teenager. But Marco was having none of that. He had told her he wanted to get to know the real Kelly Anders and she hadn't believed him. More importantly, she hadn't thought it was possible.

But nature had taken the matter out of her hands and

placed her hormones on hold while she'd been ill. Her body had been forced into pause mode and now she was faced with an entirely different situation.

The man really did care. He'd given her proof in a way that she'd never expected or anticipated.

He could just have left her—sent flowers and a card and politely wished her well. Many men would have. He hadn't. And if she thought she could just sit here and fob him off with a protective covering to her emotions that he'd already seen through...

'I don't deserve all this fuss,' she said, glancing at the sumptuous spill of summer blooms that he had bought and arranged in tall glass vases, insisting that she have them around her while she was at home.

'Kelly, you deserve much more.' He took her chin and turned her face towards him. 'Don't push me away again.'

'I'm not.'

'Trust me, *cara*. What we have is not to be cast aside. Unless, of course, you have changed your mind?'

'But what do we have?' she asked helplessly. 'I'm confused. With all the kindness you've shown me, and Frederico phoning and saying those things—'

'You mean a great deal to him,' he interrupted softly, drawing her closer. 'He does not make friends lightly. And neither do I.'

'So it's friendship we have?' she suggested quietly.

'Friendship, yes.' He nodded slowly. 'And it could be more. If you would allow it.'

Kelly had no answer for that. How could any kind of relationship grow in the time they had allotted? And even if their friendship survived separation, how long would it be before she saw either Marco or Frederico again? Her life was here in England, theirs in Italy. Long-distance relationships didn't work. Everyone knew that, so why should theirs be an exception?

'Kelly, there are no guarantees for happiness,' he continued softly. 'Let's take one day at a time, as nature intended.'

How was it that he always convinced her of something she just couldn't work out for herself? When she was with him, it all seemed so right. Yet, sometimes, when she was on her own, and in a moment of painful clarity, she could hardly believe she had let things go so far. She was falling in love with a man who would be returning to Italy soon and out of her life for ever.

His fingers wove through the waves of her hair that she had mustered up the strength to shampoo and condition this afternoon. All through her sickness Marco had carefully sponged and combed it, ignoring the dishevelled sight she must have presented. Now his fingers plucked at the soft, glossy thickness curving round her heart-shaped face.

His eyes devoured her as she leaned against him. A hard knot formed in her chest and lower, heat pooled between her thighs like a warm sea of yearning.

She raised her fingers to his face and touched the hard, coarse bristle of his dark beard. For the first time in days her body felt whole again, and with it came a rush of physical need so great that he saw it in her eyes.

'*Cara*,' he muttered, 'don't look at me that way.'

Her cheeks flamed. 'I can't help it.'

He drew her close, his fingers tightening over her arms. 'Be careful of what you say, Kelly...'

She shook her head wordlessly as her hands slipped around his neck and she raised herself to the kiss that she so desperately needed. It came, restrained at first, as he himself was restrained. As though he was holding himself on such a tight leash that the smallest movement would break it. But then her body melted into him and her mouth opened like a flowering bloom that made it impossible for him to refuse.

And all at once she was captured in his arms and she clutched mindlessly at the cool crisp cotton of his shirt, her fingers weaving their way erratically into the thick, black mane of hair that fell over his collar.

Her tongue entwined with his and he shuddered, bringing her against him so hard that for a brief second the breath left her body. Desire circled in her like a brewing storm and she could feel his heartbeat, pounding against her breastbone.

This wasn't planned, a little voice wailed inside her head. This wasn't supposed to happen. Kelly opened her eyes briefly to the intense blue stare that was raking over her. And as if in mutual, silent agreement they sank into the cushions of the sofa, Marco's hand drawing over her shoulders and back to pull her beside him. Winding her limbs around his, she arched her neck for his kisses as his mouth moved over her jaw and neck and slowly, hotly to the bare expanse of skin below, protected only by the flimsy top that she had put on after showering.

Her breast was suddenly cushioned by his hand as it curved over the lacy bra and delved into the delicate silk, his fingers soon finding their way to the clasp and loosening it. A little gasp caught in her throat as his head moved downward and he peeled away the four small buttons that fastened her blouse at the front.

She wriggled it off as his lips moved over her breasts, exposed in the soft light of the lamp, their peaks reaching for his attention as if they had been waiting just for his touch. And with a lack of self-consciousness that terrified her, she arched in pleasure at the movement of his tongue, softly flicking and nibbling the erect buds with exquisite tenderness. Burying his head in her breasts, she pillowed it softly with shaking hands, his hair running through her fingers as he moved lower to the gathering heat in her stomach.

Sensing her delight, his fingers tugged at the waistband of her sarong skirt and, front opening, it slipped away from her limbs with ease. Responding, her hands went to his shirt and the full, tensed muscle of his arms, and he slipped it off, lifting himself away for a few seconds to slide off the leather belt around his waist.

She smelt his maleness and yearned for the pleasure that it promised. Her hands groped at the opening of his chinos and found his incredible arousal. Her heart seemed to stand still as he paused, kicking off the rest of his clothing and letting them tumble on the floor, his nakedness like a shot of adrenaline to her raw system.

'Kelly,' he whispered on a shattered groan as he lifted her against him, the last barrier of her fragile panties remaining. But his attempt to remove them was neither swift nor clumsy as he savoured her body as though supping from a feast set for a king.

His eyes slid over her breasts and the flat plane of her abdomen, lingering on the strip of ivory silk that covered the moist, throbbing place beneath. His fingers flowed over the length of her legs gently splashed with a faint summer tan. Then he cupped her breasts and she groaned, helpless to hide her pleasure as his touch.

'You are so beautiful, *mi amore*,' he said raggedly, teasing the skin around her erect nipples with butterfly kisses. 'The more I see of you, the more I want you.'

Before she had time to think she cried out in a groan of barely suppressed need and his fingers wound themselves into the lacy silk at her hips and slid it over her thighs. In nakedness she lay before him, her body throbbing. And with hunger that burnt in his eyes, he pulled her to him and she wrapped herself around his hard, strong limbs.

Then he pressed his mouth breathlessly to hers and she finally parted her lips to say his name and beg him to take her. A wish that he fulfilled without hesitation as a dark flush enveloped his features and the raw and physical need within him broke loose, sweeping them both into mindless ecstasy.

He stared into her eyes for one swift moment and met her incredible high with a look of possessive tenderness that swirled into waves of deepest ultramarine. Then suddenly he was inside her and she moved with him as though their union had been ordained from the beginning of time. Heart thumping, pulse racing, a starburst of light and colour swept over her, filling every corner of her mind and body.

An agonized groan escaped his lips and a soft cry slid from hers. They clung, all the pent-up yearning of the last few months exploding into a climax of exquisite joy. With her limbs folded around him, he held her, her fingers unconsciously working over his scalp as the breath left her body and she finally shuddered to stillness.

Marco sank beside her soon after, his arm outstretched over her, his head fallen briefly on her shoulder. Kelly moved to kiss the thick black hair, inhaling the cologne that filtered up from the damp, glossy waves. And a wave of tenderness filled her that surprised her almost as much as the last few shattering minutes had done.

He must have been feeling the same, too, because he pulled her against his chest, swathing her in a bear hug of an embrace.

'Oh, Kelly, I was so certain I could resist you,' he muttered into her hair, kissing her lightly. 'You have only just begun to get better—'

'Shh,' she murmured, bringing his head up between her hands. 'Don't say anything now. It's too perfect.'

'Do you mean that?'

She nodded, curling beside him, and he hugged her gently against his chest.

'Are you cold?'

'No, not as long as your arms are around me.'

Unselfconsciously, she slewed one long slender leg around his and his fingers drifted down it, easing her into the shape of his body.

'You feel part of me,' he whispered, stroking the wet hair from her face as they relaxed on the pillowed cushions. 'Another arm, leg, heart...all so familiar...'

'Strange, isn't it?'

'You feel that, too?'

She nodded and the breath jammed in her lungs as his hand found the damp jut of her hip, settling there, the pad of his thumb trailing downward. Too far downward for decency's sake, and something fierce and powerful began to throb again inside her that she couldn't ignore.

'*Cara*?' he muttered as his body stiffened, and she knew that whatever had begun tonight was not about to stop.

'Touch me,' she pleaded in a voice half-strangled by surprise and need, and he touched her, finding her moist, and a groan echoed up from his chest as he unwound himself and brought her astride him, her thighs shackled to his in a pulsating grip.

'What are you doing to me?' His fingers tracked over her breasts so erotically she wanted to scream, and she might well have done if he hadn't cried out first. Arching and holding her still, he began to move and her head dropped back and she moaned aloud as he drove into her, lifting her, until she uttered a shuddering cry, lost in a world light years away from earth.

Not far enough, though, to be unaware of his own unique delight, following hers by a matter of seconds, so that they collapsed finally into each others arms, exhausted and satiated.

For a long while they lay curled, silent and at peace. The kind of peace that came after a storm. He had released some smouldering power inside her that, at thirty years of age, she had never even dreamed she possessed. Whether or not he knew, too, she wasn't certain. But she didn't care. Not while she lay in his arms on a hot summer night, naked and blissfully fulfilled.

A situation which, of course, couldn't last. Not even for another hour, as the marina clubhouse clock struck midnight and she stirred in his arms.

'It's late,' she murmured, unwrapping herself as he blinked tiredly and scooped back his hair. 'You must go home.'

'Don't worry,' he coaxed her. 'They will be asleep.' He

grinned, a dark, sexy grin that had her wanting to beg to make him stay. But she was too aware of the situation with Frederico and Isabella to do that.

'I'll find my robe,' she said, and swung her legs from the sofa, sliding the linen throw from under them and wrapping it around her.

He looked up at her with seductive, gorgeous eyes. 'What?'

'We are not just *friends* now, are we?'

'Not just friends,' she repeated, and he slid his long, muscular brown legs over the side of the sofa, reaching up to catch her hand.

She gave a little sigh at his naked beauty as his heavy lids fluttered wide and he grasped her hand. 'Kelly, we failed to use contraception.'

She nodded. 'We didn't think.'

'I should have taken steps—'

'I'll take the emergency Pill tomorrow,' she assured him, and gave a little shudder as his eyes seemed to bore deeply inside her. 'Use the bathroom if you like. Second on the right along the hall.'

And she fled.

It was half past twelve by the time Marco left and sleep was impossible so Kelly showered and settled back on the sofa and hugged the throw to her chest, inhaling his scent. She fell asleep there and didn't wake until morning, the sun streaming in through the blinds and casting ladders of light around the room.

He phoned early, before work, and told her he would call in that evening. She tried to protest that she was fine, but he had his way in the end.

'Just for an hour,' he told her. 'I can't drive by and not stop.'

'Only an hour, then,' she agreed, thinking of Frederico and Isabella. 'As much as I want to see you, so does your son.'

Halfway through the morning she had stomach cramps and her period arrived, taking care of last night's event. And when he called at six-thirty that evening, he brought fresh flowers and a sinful box of chocolates to tempt her appetite.

They sat on the patio and held hands in the soft evening air. The minutes flew by and she wished they had longer. But her conscience pricked and she made him go just before eight.

Her period stopped overnight. The sickness, she decided, had kicked in to her hormones. But by Friday, she felt well enough to return to work and she phoned Marco in the morning to say so.

'Monday,' he told her firmly, 'and not before.'

'But I'm well now!'

'Good. Then I'll take you out to eat tomorrow evening.'

'I feel a fraud,' she complained. 'If I can go out with you, I can work today.'

'I'll call for you at seven.'

'But—'

'No buts. It's a date.'

Their first real date, Kelly realized. And for the rest of the evening she pampered herself and hung out the blue silk dress, shivers running down her spine as she thought of tomorrow and what it would be like to be wined and dined by her lover.

It was fantastic, as she had known it would be. They ate Italian, in a little country restaurant that Antonio had recommended. The lasagna was superb and the sauce to die for, followed by sorbet that melted on her tongue. But just seeing him opposite her, meeting his eyes across the table, did much more for her than the food.

He looked devastating in a deep grey suit and a shirt so white that it gleamed as pristinely as his teeth as he smiled and licked his lips with the edge of his tongue. His black hair was smoothed back to the nape of his neck and his eyes flickered with an amazing blue light. Across the table she smelt his cologne and it did unmentionable things to her insides.

She was so relieved she had decided to wear the blue silk dress. It was a semi-formal occasion and all the women in the restaurant looked sophisticated, even though the evening was hot and humid. The silk was cool against her softly tanned skin and her hair, a little longer than it usually was at this time of year, curved in a short bob around her face. Her violet eyes had regained their depth of vitality. They shone naturally and their black fringes enhanced their lustre.

They ate and talked and laughed so much that she felt as though they had known each other a lifetime. And after they finished their meal with cappuccinos, they strolled in the beautiful floodlit gardens, hand in hand. A stream trickled lazily over mossy stones and they stood on the little wooden bridge, watching the flurry of water.

He drew her into his arms and kissed her and her body ached for more. For much more. But she knew that was impossible, his priority, as it should be, his son.

'He has a friend sleeping over tonight,' Marco whispered as he teased a lock of hair behind her ear. 'And Isabella and her friend will, no doubt, discuss their boyfriends while I am out of the way. So I have every excuse to be late.'

'No,' she protested, her fingers weaving their way into his hair. 'I don't want that. You've been away from them too much while I've been sick.'

'They want to see you, *cara*.'

'Do they?'

'Very much.'

'Maybe we can spend some time together soon.'

Marco smiled. 'Come to Canzone with us for a weekend. It is almost finished. And the pond is complete.'

'For a weekend?' she repeated, her heart racing fast.

'You don't approve?'

Kelly gave a little shrug. 'Well…yes…but—'

'Then it's settled. Before Frederico returns to Italy.'

'When is that?' she asked, a sudden hitch in her voice.

'In four weeks' time. It was arranged before we came to England. He returns to stay with his grandmother. It will be the longest time we have been separated.'

A little shiver of ice went down her spine. 'He'll miss you.'

'Yes. And I him.' He smiled softly in the dusk that clung to them like a sudden shadow. 'You are very lovely tonight, *mi amore*,' he whispered, bending to kiss her. 'I want to unwrap you from this soft, silky dress and hold you in my arms again.'

He almost destroyed her with his soft whisperings and her resolve very nearly crumbled as the thought of his naked body lying beside her was an overwhelming temptation. But she held onto her vow not to interfere with his family commitments and she kissed him back with subdued passion.

'We'll find time soon,' she murmured, and his tongue flicked out to the corners of her mouth and his kiss was deep and long. His hands moved over her with unbearable tenderness and she remembered the way he had driven her crazy the night before last. And how natural it would be to fall asleep in his arms once more.

Slowly she pulled away and gave a little sigh. 'We must go.'

'I don't want to.'

'Neither do I.' She kissed him softly and took his hand and they strolled back to the car, arms linked, hip to hip, in the misty summer damp air, the pink-grey sky darkening behind them to indigo.

Kelly's initial burst of energy on Monday morning lasted until lunchtime. She hadn't realized just how weak she felt until Joanne came in with her afternoon list. And it was long. Her sigh must have given her away because Joanne immediately looked concerned.

'We did try to ease you back in,' she said worriedly, 'but Dr Collins is on call and Dr Dallori's gone to a possible ectopic. Which leaves just you and Dr Saunders holding the fort. I could try to whittle a few down to Becky.'

'No.' Kelly shrugged. 'I'll get my second wind after this coffee.'

Joanne smiled and walked to the door. 'Oh, by the way. A patient of yours, Tania Farlow, called in early this morning. She wanted to see you, but she was streets ahead of time. We'd only just opened the doors.'

'I thought she was in hospital.' Kelly frowned. 'She must have been discharged.'

'She did look a bit poorly,' Joanne said. 'She had a cast on her arm. She wanted to see you or Dr Dallori. There was an older man with her, her father probably.'

'I'll ring her flat. Thanks, Jo. And the coffee's very welcome.'

When she had finished her drink, she rang Tania's number, not really expecting an answer. But someone picked up and Kelly recognized it as Lyn, Tania's flatmate. 'Tania's not here,' she said hesitantly. 'She's gone home to her parents. Her dad came down and I had to tell him where she was. He persuaded the hospital to let her go back to Sussex with them.'

'Oh, that's a relief,' Kelly sighed.

There was a pause and Lyn said quietly. 'You really care about Tania, don't you?'

'I care that a bully has the power to ruin her life, yes,' Kelly said heavily.

There was a long silence before Lyn replied. 'He's already picked on another first-year. She moved into his place while Tania was away. It makes me sick, but what can I do? Garry can be a real charmer. I should know. I went out with him, too. But I was no use to him. He dropped me as soon as Tania came on the scene.'

After her conversation with Lyn, Kelly felt unsettled and angry. The man was a parasite, yet no one seemed to be able to do anything about him. And now, it seemed, he had another victim to replace Tania.

Four patients later and only a quarter of the way through her list, Kelly was still thinking about what Lyn had told her. But it wasn't until much later in the week that an idea sprang to mind. An idea that she needed to discuss with Marco, which gave her a perfectly valid excuse to ask him to bring Fredrico and Isabella to lunch on Sunday.

CHAPTER TEN

IT WAS a heartbreakingly beautiful evening. A fine mist lifted up from the marina and a golden sun was setting against a cloudless blue sky. Marco stretched out on the lounger, his long body at ease on the cushions as a faint scent of bonfire crept into the air.

Kelly had just filled the dishwasher with Isabella and now they were relaxing in the garden. Her home-made carrot and broccoli soup and Sunday roast chicken, followed by fresh fruit cocktail and ice cream, had been an unqualified success.

Frederico had paid her the highest compliment. 'Just like my grandmother's cooking,' he had said with a beaming smile as he had eaten every crumb on his plate.

'I could get used to such luxury,' Marco had added, a gleam in his eye as he'd licked his full lips and smiled mischievously.

'Me, too.' Isabella had nodded as they'd sat at the table in Kelly's dining room. 'You will have to teach me the secret of your...what do you call it, your Sunday roast? The potatoes were delicious.'

'No secret.' Kelly laughed, though she was flattered. 'But I'm glad you enjoyed it.'

She wasn't an accomplished cook by any means, but she liked to busy herself in the kitchen when she had time. And deciding on something traditionally English had seemed to go down well.

Now, in the garden, Isabella stirred as they drank coffee. 'Frederico and I will go to watch the boats come in before dark,' she said, swinging her legs down from the lounger to the grass.

'I like it here,' Frederico protested, content to sit cross-legged by Kelly.

'You need some exercise.' Isabella grinned. 'Come on, lazy boy!'

He jumped up and charged after her and they ran into the apartment, laughing and giggling. 'We won't be late,' Isabella called from the French windows. Marco nodded and told Frederico to keep with Isabella and they disappeared.

'Oh, *cara*,' he said gruffly, hauling his long body up from the lounger. 'I have eaten but I am a starving man.' Soon she was in his arms, her body curving into his as though she had never left it.

'Kiss me,' he muttered, biting at her ear and causing her body to tremble as her lips found his in eager response. Incredible pleasure flowed through her as his mouth covered hers with a sensual longing that he didn't attempt to disguise.

They clung to one another and Kelly felt the raw, physical hunger explode inside her like a time bomb. Kept under wraps at work and in front of Frederico and Isabella, her need for him squeezed her heart like a gigantic hand.

'I miss you,' she murmured, but, still worried that they might be seen, she took his hand and led him into the apartment. The place was deserted, of course, but she felt safer inside and sank down on the sofa, pulling him beside her.

He drew her against him, his body hot and masculine under his linen shirt, and his arms felt wonderful around her. They kissed as though they had been parted for a lifetime and when eventually she took a breath, his eyes were heavy with longing. 'I have the afternoon free on Tuesday. Will you come with me to Canzone?'

'Tuesday,' she murmured, frowning. 'That's my afternoon off, too—' she began, then stopped as a smile edged his lips.

'I know.'

'But how…?'

He grinned. 'I had a word with Jamie who swapped an afternoon with a morning.'

'Did he ask why?'

'No. But Jamie is no fool.'

She let out a long sigh. 'Is that wise?'

'For a desperate man, wisdom is of no consideration.' He kissed her again. 'I can hardly keep my hands from you, *cara*. And when I see you at work—'

'Shh,' she whispered, kissing his words away. When she recalled the near-frantic frustration she felt, too, she knew that they had to be together soon.

'Lie against me,' he whispered as his hands drew her to him, and she snuggled on his chest, feeling the proud muscle ripple under her touch. His fingers softly massaged the naked skin of her arm as his hand filtered into her hair, slipping the strands between his fingers.

She closed her eyes, content to lie close to him, to accept what time they could share until they could be together again. It was wonderful to be with him and, though she had to talk to him about Tania, selfishly she grasped the few moments for herself.

'You're preoccupied today,' he murmured, sensing her mood. 'Is something troubling you?'

'Not about us,' she protested, sitting up. Sighing softly, she explained about Tania's visit to the surgery and her own subsequent conversation with Lyn.

'I see,' he said pensively. 'But being with her parents is probably the best place for her now.'

'Yes, but *he's* still on the loose and involved with another first-year.'

Marco's face darkened as he muttered an oath.

'Maybe we could talk to Tania again,' she suggested. 'One last try. If she knows that he's involved with another girl…'

'You think she still has those kind of feelings for him?' he asked in surprise.

'Yes, I do, though I'm sure she'd deny it.'

He sighed, brushing back his hair with a heavy palm. Lifting his eyes to hers he nodded slowly. 'Do you know where her parents live?'

'Our records should have a contact number.'

He nodded, stroking back her hair. 'Then we'll try again.'

Kelly raked her fingers through the softness of his hair, knowing that every day her feelings for this man deepened. She had long ago lost the power to think rationally about where they were heading. She only knew that she was grasping at every opportunity to be with him and when the end came, as it must, she would deal with the heartache in the best way she could.

'Frederico and Isabella will be back soon,' he sighed, his eyes dark with regret. 'Come here, kiss me one last time.'

The touch of his mouth on hers was slow and lingering, a kiss that promised so much, yet they both knew that time was against them. Finally he let her go and she began to straighten her clothing, and not a moment too soon as the front doorbell rang.

'*Dio*, what timing,' he muttered, sitting forward and raking a hand through his untidy hair.

'I'll go,' she offered as one black eyebrow jerked up.

'I think you had better.'

With colour flooding her cheeks, she pulled back her shoulders and went to the front door, plastering on a smile and wondering if she was going to be able to bear the wait until they were together again on Tuesday.

Monday dragged as she knew it would. Jamie had pencilled himself in for calls and Kelly confirmed her own afternoon off with the desk staff.

But Tuesday morning was fraught. Temporary residents and holidaymakers poured through the doors. Very few were emergencies, though, and Kelly was ready to leave by twelve.

Marco was still in surgery when she left and she wondered if he was as eager to see her as she was to see him. As planned, she took the old coast road to Canzone del Mare. The lane with its fringe of beautiful houses was deserted, and when she reached Antonio's villa, the sandy drive was free of vehicles. Nevertheless she parked with caution outside the house, nervously exploring the white walls and cinnamon-tiled roof with anxious eyes.

Then Marco's car entered the gate behind her and she gave a little sigh of relief as his tall figure climbed out. It was all she could do not to run towards him as a longing so fierce clenched a fist in her stomach. Seconds later they were in each other's arms and his lips sought hers with a raw desperation that she could almost taste.

'Kelly, my sweet Kelly,' he whispered as he trapped her face between his hands and need-filled eyes gazed down on her. 'The wait seemed endless...'

She had waited, too. And now that they were standing on the brink, she allowed the memories to tumble back of their first time together. Afraid this afternoon would never happen, she had sectioned them off, preparing for disappointment. But now, with his arms around her and his soft breath fanning over her face, she could really believe they were together again.

'Let's go in,' he muttered, his eyes full of fervent promise as she nodded, and in silence he unlocked the big front door. Inside, the villa smelt of paint and newness and she hardly had time to look around before Marco led her up the wide staircase.

His arm snaked around her as they entered a beautiful ivory-coloured bedroom, with wide picture windows overlooking the garden. He opened them and stepped out onto the balcony, drawing her to stand beside him.

'Look down,' he murmured, and her eyes lowered to the garden below.

She gave a small gasp of surprise. 'The pond!'

'Do you like it?'

'Oh, Marco, it's beautiful.' Delicate pink and white buds

opened amongst emerald auras of leaves in the shimmering
water that rippled smoothly from a stone fountain set in the
middle. A long bamboo pipe recycled the water to a small
pagoda on the bank. Large shiny stones peeped up from
the fronds of reeds. Shadows of tangerine fish glimmered
in the rays of sunshine spearing the water.

'Do you think Laura will like it?'

She nodded. 'I'm certain she will.'

'Thanks to you, Kelly.'

'But I didn't do anything,' she protested as he curled her
into his arms and looked down at her.

'You were the inspiration,' he whispered softly. 'One
day I shall make one for us. Would you like that, *cara*?'

Kelly stared at him. 'Marco, don't say that.'

'Why not?'

'You know why.'

He tilted her chin and searched her eyes. 'I know nothing
of the sort. Kelly, we cannot ignore the future.'

'We have the moment,' she protested weakly, her arms
folding around his neck.

'But I want more, Kelly. Don't you?'

She felt her body tremble as he gripped her. 'I can't think
that far ahead,' she admitted, the breath banking painfully
in her throat. 'All I know is that I want you. Now, this
second… The future seems another lifetime away.'

'But it does not for me,' he assured her, his expression
confirming his muttered words. 'I want you now and I want
you tomorrow. And I want you every day afterwards.'

Did he mean it? she wondered incredulously as his touch
caused a torrent of sensation to sweep down her spine. Was
he really telling her the truth? And if he was, how could
she take on board the fact that this was not just an affair
to him or a temporary resolution to the physical desire that
each had been wrestling with?

A tenderness swept over her that found the soft core of
her being, shattering her defences forged so carefully over
the years. She had sealed herself off from pain like a well-

wrapped parcel tied in sections and with the strongest of cord and glue.

And now in one sentence he had undone that parcel as he bent slowly, his head coming down and whispering soft words of Italian in her ear. His strong arms slipped under her and he carried her back into the bedroom. He lay with her on the bed and threw the covers aside, spreading her easily on the luxurious sheets as he undid the buttons of her blouse and teased it from her shoulders, fingering the soft silk with eyes that burnt her skin.

Then he paused, as if to say something, until a sudden rush of pulsing sensation charged between them like electricity and his tongue drove into her mouth with primitive yearning. A quiver of excitement ran through his hard, muscled body and he stripped off his clothes, casting them aside in careless disorder.

Her clothes seem to dance through his fingers and across the bed to the floor below. Outer garments dispensed with, her bra and panties drew a deep groan from his throat as he lifted her towards him and slipped the sliver of white silk over her hips.

The curtains shielded them from a soft breeze that blew in. A fragrance of maleness filled the air, potent enough to make her senses reel. His kisses were unrestrained, flowing over the dip of her stomach to her thighs and the soft, damp crevice between, making her eyes fly wide.

'Oh, Kelly,' he muttered as he slid against her, 'you taste like honey.'

'Don't stop,' she begged as the torment of their long wait began to coil inside her. The frenzy of their passion was wild and he held onto the last shreds of his control as she cupped his full maleness and responded to the arousal with a hunger that clawed like fire in her throat.

'I assure you, there is no risk from me,' he murmured as he took care to protect them this time.

She kissed him for his thoughtfulness, winding her limbs

around as his hand cupped the base of her spine, melding her to him.

His instinct was perfect. The racing thunder of her heart pounded with the soar of her pulse as his body quivered and he thrust and entered her. Bringing them both to a sure, swift climax, pulsing sensation racked them, until they collapsed shudderingly beside one another.

The breeze lifted the curtain again and whispered over their hot bodies as they lay exhausted in the damp sheets. Kelly gazed on the man who lay beside her. His dark lashes fluttered over deep blue pools and a tender smile touched his mouth.

'Oh, *cara*, you are a joy to behold,' he whispered, brushing her hair back from her ear with the tip of his finger as though he were touching silk. Drawing her into his chest, her palms lay on the tight black coils of hair furrowing down to the hot, damp skin beneath.

Her body trembled as she drew a breath, nestling into the arch of his neck. 'What would your brother say if he knew we were here?' she asked dreamily, and he gave a soft growl of laughter.

'He would give us his blessing,' he said easily, his breath curling over her forehead. 'Just as I give him mine with his new bride.'

Again, Kelly felt the stir of unease inside her. Did he really mean what he was saying? It was almost too painful to think about, because she had never believed anything would come of their relationship. She had already grown closer to him than she had a right to.

Yet Marco seemed unfazed as he held her in his arms and she could almost let herself believe that there was a chance.

Almost...

'This afternoon was perfect,' she whispered, trapping a sigh, as the blue orbs of desire met her own deep violet gaze.

'This afternoon is not over,' he murmured, snaking himself around her, his arms locking her to him. 'Not unless you want it to be?'

She didn't want it to be over—ever. She wasn't even going to think about leaving his arms until she had to. And as his lips covered hers once more and fire joined their bodies in a fresh wave of desire, she blocked out all thoughts that didn't enslave her to the moment.

The telephone rang and Kelly was startled awake, aware that an arm enfolded her and her back was curved against the deliciously prickly feel of rough hair.

'I'll answer it,' a husky, sleep-tinged voice murmured in her ear. And the arm around her loosened and she wriggled around to follow the body, threading her hand over the warm, naked skin that all too swiftly moved out of her reach.

In the minutes after Marco left the bed, Kelly had time to unscramble her thoughts and adjust to where she was. One of the guest rooms at Canzone del Mare. With Marco. And whatever had happened between them over the last few hours had left her body feeling utterly satiated.

She lay back and her gaze idly moved to the windows. The breeze had all but vanished and the muslin curtains hung in loose folds, their transparent whiteness penetrated by the beams of early evening sun. The room was golden and glowing. Marco had, it appeared, vanished into the little dressing room to talk on the telephone. Could it be Antonio? she wondered. Glancing at her watch, she was shocked to see it was six-thirty.

She sat up and pulled a sheet around her and was just pushing open the door to the *en suite* bathroom when Marco returned. He was wearing only close-fitting white shorts that deepened his beautiful tan and complemented the solid muscle of his athletic body.

She only had to look at him and she craved him again. Not that she could do very much about such a wanton wish. But as he came towards her, his eyes were sparkling with a deep aqua blue that reminded her of the slice of water that could be seen from the balcony of Canzone.

'That was Isabella,' he said, catching her by her waist and drawing her into his arms. He began to unfold the sheet, his dexterous fingers peeling back the layers that she had quickly wrapped around her.

'You should be at home,' she whispered, quaking at his touch.

'No. They are at the leisure centre. And will be all evening. Frederico has swimming lessons. And Isabella and her friend will bring him home.'

'Did they know you had the afternoon off today?'

He gave a little grin. 'Isabella knew.'

'You didn't—'

'I said I was coming to Canzone. She knows that I wanted to check out the finished work. Would you mind if I told her who I was with?'

She lifted her naked shoulders in a light shrug. 'I'm not sure, Marco.'

'Well, I am.'

'What do you mean?'

'Kelly, I want you to come to Italy. To meet my family.'

She gave a strained little laugh. 'You don't mean that.'

'And why not?' Marco pulled her against him, his palms running over her shoulders. 'What we have done together…how we feel…this cannot be denied.'

'And I'm not denying it,' she said quickly, almost desperately. 'But we live in two different countries, you know that.' She felt all the old stirrings of despair as she tried to find the words. 'I have my career here, in Charbourne, Marco. A job I've only just started, and as an employee of your brother. How can I take time off—?'

'Because Antonio *is* my brother, it will be easier for you.'

'I don't expect favours,' she said quietly, but her voice was firm. 'I've worked hard for this opportunity, Marco. A chance to become part of a group practice and establish myself. To fulfil the potential that I have in me to become a good family doctor. It's what I've wanted since I was a little girl. And I know I can do it. This place is perfect for me. It feels like home.' Kelly stared into his sad eyes. 'And then there is you, Marco. You have a big family back in Italy and your own practice, not to mention a wonderful son—'

'Who has become very fond of you,' he interrupted, taking her head between his hands. 'As his father is fond of you.'

'That's not enough,' she said softly.

'Enough?' he repeated in a puzzled voice. 'How can we know what is enough until we give ourselves the opportunity to discover? Italy is not such a long way away. In a few hours you could be with me, or I with you. Geographically we are not at the opposite ends of the earth.'

'We might as well be,' she answered on a sigh. 'You'll both go home, and in a little while you'll have forgotten all this.'

'No.'

'Yes.' She lifted her chin. 'Do we have to talk about this now?'

'You leave me no choice,' he said gruffly. 'There is so little time.'

'Which rather proves my point,' she murmured dryly.

For a long moment they stood there, his arms about her, and the force of his physical impact and his stubborn insistence that there was a chance for them made her momentarily weaken as she actually gave consideration to his proposal. Could they possibly sustain a long-distance relationship, commuting to see one another in holidays and the odd weekend? Even if they did, where could it lead? What could the future hold for two people set on such vastly different paths?

'Kelly…' he groaned, taking her against him and snaking his head into the crook of her neck. His mouth wove soft kisses over the skin there and her body, thankfully, began to drown the insistent noise of her mind.

Desire began to flood her limbs and the sheet finally dropped away from her as Marco's hands trickled down to her buttocks and thighs and lifted her against him. Whatever the disagreement they had had, it was as nothing as they tumbled back into the bed, hands and mouths desperate to explore, her fingers stripping away the soft white trousers that failed miserably to hide his arousal.

In thrall to the fresh surge of longing, Kelly blocked every thought out of her mind. Fire and passion ignited into feverish hunger as they began to make love again. Only this time with an edge of desperation that hadn't been there before. An edge that let the floodgates open to suspend them again in that sweet paradise where nothing mattered except fulfilment of their desire.

They were running late by the time they left Canzone. They had dressed so quickly there hadn't even been time to shower. Kelly had bundled her things into her bag and Marco had splashed water on his face in a failed attempt to wake himself up before collecting Isabella and Frederico from the leisure centre.

Kelly sat quietly in the car as he drove to the marina, her body at peace with the world but her mind too fuelled by returning sanity to be still.

All the questions tumbled back, a hundred times over, as though her brain was on overload. And Marco did nothing to help as he took her in his arms to say goodnight, pressing his mouth over hers so hungrily that her traitorous body yearned for him like a drug.

'I hope you aren't too late,' she murmured, her heart already sinking at the thought of being without him.

'Isabella will wait,' he whispered in the darkness of the early September evening. Her front door was lost in shadows. Already the nights had begun to darken, and summer would soon be a memory. 'Sleep well, little one.'

There was no reply to that, she realized, just another kiss as he finally released her and she watched him disappear into the darkness and heard the purr of his car engine as he drove away.

Indoors, the apartment seemed lost and lonely, the place that she had loved on sight when she had been first searching for a home now a pale second to the place she wanted to be.

With Marco. Lying beside him. In his arms…

After a shower, Kelly trailed into the kitchen and made herself a cold drink. She hadn't eaten for the best part of the day so she made a quick sandwich and took it into the lounge. Her body still burned from his touch, the cooling water of the shower doing nothing to remove the shuddering reflections of their love-making.

Could there really be a future for them? she wondered, knowing it was a crazy thought—but it felt so good to imagine. Her supper left untouched, she stretched out on the sofa, the cool cotton of her robe allowing her hot limbs to breathe. Her hand fell to the floor, idly stroking the rough weave of the fabric mat. Her fingers touched her bag and she was turning to lift it onto the table out of harm's way when she saw a small black wallet beside it.

She realized at once whose it was. Somehow, in the flurry of leaving Canzone, Marco must have dropped it. And she had scooped it into her bag!

With careful fingers she laid it on the coffee-table, the Italian leather soft and supple under her fingers. Should she phone him? But she couldn't. Besides being far too late, she might disturb Frederico and Isabella.

The wallet must have fallen open at some point. The clip was undone and a tiny slice of photograph poked over the edge. Kelly's eyes lay on it, making out the elbow of someone and a foot.

A dainty foot, clad in a pretty, strappy sandal. A woman's foot.

She didn't give in to temptation, not immediately. The

woman could be anyone. But a dozen assumptions, several calculated guesses and an overpowering need to know caused Kelly to open the wallet. The photograph lay inside, tucked neatly into a pocket.

For a well-thumbed photograph, the colour and clarity was still remarkable. Marco held his son tenderly, a baby nestled in the crook of his arm. The backdrop was of a beautiful garden, full of flowing vines and leafy green trees.

The family trio reclined on a rustic wooden bench. The woman's back rested against the man's. Her sandalled foot fell casually over the edge. She gazed at the camera with a soft smile, her heart-shaped face partially hidden under a wing of dark hair.

Kelly swallowed as she stared at Sophia Dallori. A mirror image of herself.

CHAPTER ELEVEN

KELLY returned the wallet on Wednesday morning, leaving it on Marco's desk with a little note. He rang through when he found it and thanked her, then asked her to meet him for lunch. She wanted to see him desperately, despite the little splinter of despair that had worked itself into her heart after seeing Sophia.

The physical ache for him won for the moment. Just to see him, to know that somehow they would be together again. She couldn't even begin to deal with the knowledge that she was Sophia's double. Not yet. Not while she missed him so much.

So they met at the harbour at a little bistro called Molly's, and when she saw his tall figure waiting for her outside, her heart flipped crazily and she forgot, briefly, the previous night's discovery.

But when they sat at one of the tables under an umbrella and held hands, she knew she could only deceive herself for so long. Was he thinking how much alike she and Sophia were? Was he waiting for her to say something Sophia might have? Do something in the same way? As they talked and ordered lunch, the lead weight of fresh doubt and jealousy swelled inside her. As his gaze went over her, she wondered what he was thinking. Was he seeing his wife sitting here beside him? Was he holding her hand?

'This weekend I'm driving Isabella and Frederico to my uncle's home in Surrey for a fortnight,' he was saying as she dragged her mind back from the incessant doubts. 'I shall stay with them until Wednesday, then return. It seems selfish to want time alone with you,' he admitted huskily, 'but I do.'

'I'll miss you,' she murmured, unable to summon up an appetite for the fresh crab sandwiches set in front of them. 'And Frederico and Isabella, too.'

'We'll all go out to dinner before Frederico goes home to Italy,' he assured her, and she looked into his eyes. 'It won't be goodbye. You'll see him again.'

'Marco, I—'

He lifted her hand and squeezed it, his blue eyes darkening. 'Don't, Kelly. Wait before you say anything. Please.'

So she didn't speak, at least not of Frederico's return to Italy or, indeed, Marco's. Instead, she managed a few mouthfuls of her lunch and all too soon they had to leave for the surgery. A pale September sun warmed the air as they strolled hand in hand to the cars parked close by. Marco snaked an arm around her waist and she wondered if anyone they knew was watching. She didn't care.

Not now, as they strolled with the closeness of lovers along the harbour wall and up the hill to the semi-deserted car park. Only a few days ago it would have been crammed with holidaymakers. Now the air was tinged by a fresher, sharper scent—a salt that reminded her of autumn and cold seas. She shivered as they stopped by her car.

'We'll be together next Wednesday,' he murmured as she looked up at him and his eyes were filled with a soft caress that tingled over her skin. 'I'll drive from Surrey after lunch. It may be late.'

'I'll be waiting,' she said weakly, and his mouth came down to cover hers and for a few sweet moments she clung to him.

Over the next two days, Kelly managed to keep focused on work. Just. The school term started the following week and there was a frantic flutter of last-minute minor problems that always surfaced in early September. Coughs and colds and sore throats materialized, but the lists weren't as hectic as those of summer.

Nights were the worst, just before sleep. Her thoughts flew wildly. She needed to talk them through. To work out in her mind what was happening to her heart. She had to speak to Meg. It wouldn't be easy, saying what she had kept secret over the past few months.

Saying it aloud was making it real. But Meg would understand. They'd relied on each other since they'd been young. And even when Meg had married Pierre and gone to live in France, they'd talked for hours on the phone.

Five years down the line, their weekly calls had become monthly rituals. And lately, as Meg had taken a bigger part in Pierre's family's handcrafted furniture business, her sister's life was never dull.

'And neither is yours, Kel,' Meg had reminded her on their last meeting at Christmas. Kelly had flown over and stayed for the holiday at their Paris apartment. 'You've never stopped chasing that career of yours. Ambition has always snapped at your heels.'

It had been true. And Kelly had known it.

Amidst a sea of Christmas presents and an endless flow of callers, they'd had few precious moments alone. Not until Pierre and the children had been in bed and the elegant city centre apartment had returned to its former tranquillity.

'Heard from Dad?' Meg had asked nonchalantly as they'd sat with glasses of mulled wine, curled on the big scatter cushions by the fire.

'A letter in summer.' Kelly had shrugged. 'He said he'd try to fly over from the States.'

Meg had nodded, grinning. 'Yeah, I had one of those, too.'

They'd laughed together then, making light of their father's infrequent correspondence, but Kelly had known Meg was disappointed. Luckily Pierre's mother and father doted on their grandchildren and they hadn't missed out on the ties that bound family close.

Kelly smiled at the memory of the bittersweet memories they'd shared that Christmas night. She would have to wait until the next holiday to see Meg again. Maybe Christmas or New Year. But right now she wanted to hear Meg's voice.

So on Friday evening, she phoned.

'Kel! What's happened?' Meg demanded at once. 'Why haven't you phoned?'

'Where to start,' Kelly sighed, sinking down onto the stool beside her. 'Actually, Meg—'

'You've met someone!' Meg exclaimed, apparently knowing Kelly better than she knew herself. 'Who is he?'

With Meg's intuition tuned as keenly as a radio antenna, Kelly had no choice but to blurt out the whole story. How she had first met Marco and Frederico at the surgery and how their relationship had developed over the last couple of months.

By the time she came breathlessly to the end, she knew she couldn't be making a lot of sense. From deeply distrusting Marco's motives initially to having an affair with him was a leap by anyone's imagination. And when she came to explain about Sophia's photograph, she felt she sounded insanely jealous, which was ridiculous, of course.

'And because you *think* you bear a resemblance to his first wife,' Meg asked with a similar note of suspicion in her normally sweet voice, 'you think he's trying to replace *her*—with *you*?'

'Well, yes,' Kelly faltered, adding swiftly, 'It's possible, isn't it?'

'You're grasping at straws, Kel.'

'What do you mean?'

'I mean, he's behaving perfectly normally if what you say is true about looks. Lots of men go for the same type. For instance, Pierre's a leg man. All his girlfriends were beanpoles with legs the length of planks. But he married *me*, not them. And if you look a bit like Sophia, my guess is that Marco is attracted to tall, slim, attractive brunettes.'

'But she is—*was*—exceptionally lovely,' Kelly protested, 'and he obviously adored her. What if he's trying
to recapture the past, Meg? I couldn't live up to another
woman's image, especially one who was so perfect.'

'So you really do like him,' her sister said breathily. 'I
mean, if you've considered the relationship in that depth?'

Kelly was silent for a moment, then heaved a sigh. 'I'm
so confused, I don't know what I feel. Everything was going—'

'*According to plan*,' Meg butted in, repeating the words
that had become Kelly's catch-phrase since she'd been a
little girl. 'Kelly, you drive me crazy sometimes, you're so
passionately organized! Look, sometimes we have to take
a gamble in life. That's where the excitement comes in.
The uncertainty. The fun.'

'I hate uncertainty, Meg,' Kelly protested gently. 'I like
to be in control of my life. Don't you?'

'Have you forgotten that Pierre is French?' Meg reminded her indignantly. 'And ours was a holiday romance,
if you recall.'

'Yes, I remember,' Kelly agreed lamely, realizing Meg
had a point.

'I don't say it's been easy,' Meg continued stiffly. 'I've
had to adapt to another language and culture. I'd only ever
visited France on holiday. But it's fun and exciting because
life is still a challenge.'

Kelly bit her lip. 'It's just that I've begun to carve a
career here in Charbourne. Then just as I do so—'

'You fall in love.'

'I didn't say I had.'

'You don't need to.' Meg's voice softened. 'Oh, Kel,
don't be too hard on him or yourself. Your standards have
always been miles too high. After Dad left us, you took on
the world for our sakes, bless you. But you don't need to
look after me or Mum any more. You're a free spirit. You
can do whatever you like.'

Had she really done what Meg had just said? Kelly reflected with some surprise. She hadn't seen it that way, consciously. If she had done battle on their behalf, it had only been to help Mum through her cancer and to keep Meg from running wild.

Perhaps her standards had seemed high, saving every penny and budgeting like a lunatic and making Meg do the same. But frugality had been the only way to survive and her dreams had been like liferafts of hope in the stormy sea of everyday survival after Dad had vanished.

Just as her protective instincts had kicked in then, so had they screamed out to her when she'd seen the photograph of Marco's wife. And they'd been on red alert ever since. It had suddenly come home that even if she seriously considered Marco's suggestion to continue their relationship after his return to Italy, Sophia would always be there, in the background, as she was now, in Marco's wallet positioned next to his heart.

Marco was looking for a replacement wife. Which was the real reason why he had pursued her so determinedly from the start. The mystery had been solved. She had been puzzled and flattered by his persistence, but now she knew why—even if he didn't seem to. She fitted Sophia's blueprint and Marco had been drawn towards it from the very beginning.

But following the role model of a beloved late wife was something she couldn't handle. Even if all the other problems attached to their relationship were solved, this one was insurmountable.

With difficulty, Kelly shifted the focus of the conversation. At last, after hearing all Meg's news, Kelly rang off with a promise to call again soon. As she replaced the phone, she knew that she had come to a decision. She had decided on the course of her life before she had Marco. And she would survive after he returned to Italy.

Still, she missed them all while they were in Surrey.

And if she had thought it would be easier now that she'd made up her mind, she was wrong. In Marco's absence her

hunger for him sharpened rather than dulled. And on
Monday the surgery seemed desolate without him.

Her pulse had always sped as she'd passed his room and
force of habit caused the same reaction, only to slow and
plummet as she glanced at the empty chair and unusually
tidy desk. A faint fragrance trickled out that was Marco.
Indefinable and yet his. It melted her nerve ends as she
inhaled it and walked swiftly away to her room.

Mrs Frost was waiting for her. 'It's my diabetes, Dr
Anders,' the elderly lady pleaded as she made herself comfortable in the chair. 'Your girls fitted me in. Dr Dallori
took a blood sample last week and he revised my diet. I do
tend to go off the rails a bit sometimes. He's so easy to
talk to. I just thought I'd come back for a reassuring chat
to see that I'm doing everything right now.' She looked
around the room. 'He's not here, then?'

'He's not in surgery until Thursday, I'm afraid.' Kelly
hid a smile at her patient's obvious disappointment.

'What a shame! I thought he'd like to know how much
better I feel. I'm really not looking forward to him leaving,
you know.'

A sentiment that Kelly's heart echoed as she took yet
another blood sample and attempted to discover whether
Mrs Frost was keeping to her diet and medication. The
conversation pivoted back and forth from diabetes to
Marco, but finally Kelly assured her all was well and Mrs
Frost departed.

Hannah appeared then, with baby Patrick, and Kelly ad-
ministered his immunization. He offered a sudden bleat of
indignation but a few moments later, as Kelly trapped his
little fingers with her own, his smile was dazzling.

'How are you?' Kelly asked Hannah as she tucked
Patrick back into the buggy.

'We had a full night's sleep last night.' She smiled. 'And
my breasts are back to normal again. And after I last spoke
to you, I realized how much Patrick's birth had worried
Phillip. Anyway, we talked things over and agreed that cir-

cumcision will go on the back burner for now. We want to enjoy our son, not fight over him.'

'A good move.' Kelly nodded as Hannah rose and pushed the buggy to the door.

'Sometimes you get trapped into focusing on the wrong things,' Hannah said as she opened it. 'I was so preoccupied with the feeding and breast problems, I was beginning to forget I had a husband.' She smiled brightly. 'Anyway, thanks, Dr Anders. See you for his next booster.'

Kelly watched Hannah walk away, aware of Marco's silent room just a few feet away and Hannah's words ringing in her ears.

Focusing on the wrong things...

Somehow she had lost focus of her life with Marco in it. And somehow, no matter how painful it was, she had to restore it again.

Kelly found it hard to pay attention to anything until Wednesday. And then she was so nervous at the thought of seeing Marco that evening that she went through her surgery with determined, meticulous care.

The ploy worked well, but she felt exhausted at the end of the day. She'd struck all her outstanding jobs from her list, brought her correspondence bang up to date and even sorted out her pending tray. By six she was ready to leave, and Michelle and Joanne at the desk gave her slightly curious glances as she offered to do extra visits.

'I don't think there are any.' Michelle shrugged, glancing down the list. 'Dr Saunders and Dr Collins took them earlier.'

'Oh, well, never mind.' Kelly brushed her offer aside with an embarrassed grin. 'It looks like an early night.'

'Make the most of it.' Joanne laughed. 'The lull won't last long.'

'See you tomorrow, then.' Kelly slipped her bag over her shoulder.

'Dr Dallori's in tomorrow,' Michelle said cheerfully.

'The place doesn't seem the same without him, does it?
And it's October next month. Dr Antonio's back on the
sixth.'

Kelly managed a nod, then hurtled to her car. She struggled not to think how it would be in October when Marco's
stay came to an end. But by the time she found herself
home, the palms of her hands were damp and she felt
slightly nauseous.

She flew to the shower, stripped off and stood underneath
it. But even here she wasn't free from her memories of
Marco as they tormented her mind with visions of his lean,
hard body, the way his skin smelt as he nuzzled his face
against her. His eyes, as they gazed at her, the way her
head rested on his chest and she'd listened to the strong
beat of his heart.

And that was the way he found her, soaking wet, her
body aching for him, wrapped in a fluffy white towel as
she answered the ring of the doorbell.

'I'm early,' he apologized, scraping a hand through his
hair, and she reached out to drag him in.

'I've missed you.' In his arms she was whole again, both
in body and mind, and he kissed her with fire on his lips
as the front door closed behind him.

'Me, too,' he groaned as he parted the towel from her
breasts and it slipped to the floor and his hands went over
her wet, warm body with unbearable tenderness, pressing
her against his clothes and dampening his dark blue shirt.

It was seconds before his clothes were discarded, too.
They stood in the shower together, the sweet torment of
their separation like a match to the flame. He made love to
her there and Kelly's eyes filled with tears.

Luckily, the water hid them.

She didn't know what they were for. Only that she
needed to shed them. Tears that Marco finally transformed
into sighs of sweet and utter contentment.

*   *   *

They ate out whilst Frederico and Isabella were in Surrey, savouring intimate, cosy suppers at little bistros rather than restaurants. But most of the time they spent lazing by the swimming pool at Marco's, long evenings bathing in the soft September air and tepid water, the presence of autumn passing unnoticed as an Indian summer held everyone in thrall.

Waking to Marco's strong, naked body wrapped around her was what she loved best. That first moment of consciousness, knowing he was beside her and had been all night, the whorls of crisp black hair compressed against her back. The deep rise and fall of his chest in sleep and heavy solidness of his limbs as one leg trapped her and curved her slender form around to him.

It was a joy that needed no other diversion. Even work was a distraction before they were home again, making love sometimes before eating, their craving for one another the fiercest hunger of all. Salads, fresh foods and fruits comprised their meals. Marco said he felt as though they were living on a tropical island. And she went along with that. Not allowing herself to think of October, as they spent every hour available together.

The weather held and they went to the beach and found little coves and explored all along the shoreline. There were no tourists now and it was heaven. Their own little paradise as the soft, wet sand and salt-tinged air lifted the evenings to a delirious contentment. They walked for miles and found shells and driftwood for Frederico.

Then, on the day before Marco drove up to Surrey for Frederico and Isabella, they found an older man waiting for them as they arrived at surgery.

'I'm Eric Farlow,' he said, stepping out to greet them as they entered Reception. 'My daughter Tania is a patient here.'

'Tania?' Kelly looked into the man's face and nodded. 'We had no forwarding address after she left hospital. Dr

Dallori and I were going to make enquiries at the university—'

'They wouldn't have given it,' Eric interrupted softly. 'I asked that our address be withheld, for obvious reasons.'

'Is Tania still with you?' Marco asked.

'She is.'

Marco nodded slowly. 'I'm sorry we could not do more for your daughter.'

'Oh, but you did. Tania took your advice and told us the whole story.'

'She did?' Kelly asked in surprise.

'Yes, and I have no intention of letting that man get away with what he did. Neither shall I stand by and allow him to ruin my daughter's future. Or anyone else's, come to that. The police have spoken to Tania's young friend, Lyn. There is another girl, too, who is prepared, fortunately, after what I told her, to give evidence against him.' He glanced up at Marco. 'Would you be prepared to give statements, too?'

'Without hesitation.' Marco nodded.

'We'll do anything we can to help,' Kelly added. 'How is Tania?'

He gave a tired smile. 'Her cast has been removed but her wrist is still painful. She broke a bone that damaged the radial nerve. But she is returning to university, nevertheless.'

'Good news.' Marco smiled.

'Again, we should like to express our appreciation,' Eric said, stretching out his hand and taking Kelly's then Marco's.

'Amazing,' Kelly sighed as they watched him walk away. 'Tania did actually listen to us.'

'*Si*,' Marco said, his expression far away until he looked down at her. 'Now, before we set tongues wagging, we must hurry in different directions. Until this evening, *cara*…?'

She smiled at his tease, aware that they were indeed

drawing curious glances from the desk. But, then, they had every morning as they had arrived together. Once she would have been concerned, but now she really didn't care.

'I liked the man,' Marco murmured later that day as he stretched out beside Kelly on a steamer chair by the swimming pool. 'God knows what I would have done if she had been a daughter of mine.'

They had been discussing Tania and her father in the first slight chill of the month and Kelly had wrapped her beach robe around her as they lay in the last of the sunshine.

'You would have probably done the same,' Kelly responded, glancing at him as he rested his head back on the seat, a frown furrowing his forehead. 'You're a good father, Marco.'

He tugged her gently against him, tenderly kissing her mouth as the sun melted over them in warm waves. His body was a deep golden brown broken only by the light blue swimming trunks that fitted sleekly around his slim hips. 'Drive up with me to Surrey tomorrow, Kelly.'

She had planned to go back to her apartment tomorrow, the inside of which she had barely seen in the last two weeks. Not that she regretted a minute of staying with Marco. Though she had missed Frederico and Isabella's company, the days had flown past.

'Will you?' he persisted.

'Oh, Marco, I don't think so.' She had already begun to adjust her mind to being without him. But when he looked at her, his eyes smouldering with that deep blue that made the dark fringes seem like fans to the fires of his soul, Kelly's body ached with desire.

'Why, Kelly,' he demanded gruffly, 'will you not come with me? I want you to meet my family. My uncle and his wife and my cousin Gabrielle and her husband. They are wonderful people. I know you would like them.'

'I'm sure I would,' Kelly agreed, lowering her eyes.

'I want you to meet *all* of the Dallori family,' he insisted swinging down his legs and grasping her hands. 'Mamma Luca, Pietro, Roberto, their wives and children—everyone I want you to come to Italy, *cara*. Yet when I speak abou this, you draw away from me. I don't understand.'

'Marco, we've talked about this,' she argued, trying t withdraw her hands, but he held on to them tightly. 'Wh can't we just enjoy the time we have?'

'Because it's not enough.'

'It has to be.'

'Kelly, you are a stunningly beautiful woman. I desir you deeply. But there is much more to our relationship tha sex. We have so much in common. Our careers, ou tastes—we are compatible and you must know this.'

'Marco, if it means that much to you, I can come to Ital for a holiday—'

'Not a holiday,' he interrupted shortly, his brows com pressed above splintering blue eyes. 'I ask for much more.

She felt heat flow up into her face and clog in her throa as she loosened her hands. 'It wouldn't work,' she sai simply, suddenly aware that tears were balancing on he lids.

'But why? Life is a compromise, Kelly. Are we so rigi that we cannot bend to make ourselves happy?'

She had heard the same words from Meg, and she ha already turned all the possibilities over in her mind. Bu she always came back to Sophia.

He stood up and came towards her, pulling her into hi arms, his chin against her cheek as he breathed a deep sigh 'How could I have been so clumsy?' he growled, his breath caressing her skin. 'I was angry—distressed—that I coul not have my way.' He held her tight again, his body shud dering against her. 'Forgive me, *cara*.'

'There's nothing to forgive,' she mumbled, pressing he mouth against his shoulder. 'Make love to me, Marco.'

His body tensed as he lifted her and carried her to th

bedroom, laying her on the bed to slide the belt from her robe and stare down at her naked body.

'You are beautiful, *cara*. More beautiful than any woman have known.' He said the words with husky passion, but as he said them her mind began the old torture. Doubts crowding in like poison darts intent on spoiling her happiness. More beautiful than Sophia? More beautiful than the wife you loved and lost?

And she didn't even have the courage to voice them. Couldn't bring herself to ask or even hint at what was in her heart. And what, if she was truthful, was the real reason for her tears? Tears that had come so unexpectedly this evening.

They had sprung from her eyes so readily because she knew that he had left out the most important factor in his summing-up of their relationship. That one small word that made every woman's vocabulary complete. Without it, there was no future, no choice. But, then, how could she expect this man to love her? A pale shadow of his first—and only—love, Sophia.

CHAPTER TWELVE

THE fleeting regret that she was not accompanying Marco the following day quickly vanished in a giddy wave of nausea that swept over Kelly the next morning. Even Marco's puzzled expression at her reluctance to share breakfast by the pool couldn't persuade her to nibble at toast or drink the oranges he had squeezed especially for her.

And although she bitterly missed his company after he had gone and she had returned to her own apartment, the unpleasant sensation that she was still aboard a cross-channel ferry in a rough sea and rising storm continued unabated.

So she bathed and washed her hair and went to bed before ten and spent Sunday quietly, trying not to think of the consequences of what she might have done.

On Monday, Marco came into her room before surgery. 'Did you miss me?' he asked, closing the door and walking to her desk with a long and determined stride so that she was smiling as he took her wrist and pulled her into his arms.

'You know the answer to that,' she murmured as he rained kisses over her cheeks and in her hair. 'How is Frederico?'

The change of subject didn't help as he grinned, his eyes mischievously devouring her. 'He missed you. Almost as much as I did.'

'Marco—' she protested, but he took her hand and led her into the little treatment room where they could not be seen. 'We'll take the boat out again this weekend,' he told her animatedly, as he wrapped her in his arms. 'Just you and Frederico and I. Isabella is seeing her friend, but she will join us in the evening for dinner. We shall have a wonderful day—the three of us—'

'Marco, I may be on call,' she interrupted, attempting to hide the swaying unease inside. Since she had woken, it had been all she could do to keep down the dry biscuit she had forced herself to eat. And Marco seemed to be rushing ahead, making plans that he hadn't even discussed with her.

'No, Jamie is,' he said in a voice so low and sexy that she couldn't bring herself to argue the point. But as she gave a half-hearted nod, he cupped her face in his hands. 'What is wrong, Kelly? Are you well? You are so pale. And those lovely eyes are not shining.'

'I'm fine,' she answered quietly. 'A little tired, perhaps.'

'You need a holiday,' he murmured, and she realized it was probably the worst thing she could have said. 'A place in the sun,' he continued, as though drawing a picture that he had no intention of letting her forget. 'A beautiful island where dreams come true, where we could make *our* dreams come true, *cara*.' He turned his head to one side. 'I said before I would not settle for a few weeks' holiday, but now I am a desperate man. I've had time to think while being away from you, and I am willing to accept whatever you want or desire.'

'Marco, please, it's not like that,' she insisted, uncertain herself what she was trying to say. She knew only that she mustn't be drawn into emotions she just couldn't handle. She moved away, resisting his strength as he tried to hold onto her.

'All right,' he growled, dragging her back into his arms with a look of defeat. 'I won't press the point. But being without you for two days, I have withdrawal symptoms. You see how lost I am without your company?'

She smiled softly. 'I'm sure you had a wonderful time.'

'It would have been better with you by my side, *cara*.' He shrugged heavily. 'But I forgot, I am not allowed to tell you this.'

She pretended she hadn't heard as the telephone rang and she escaped to lift the receiver, grateful to Joanne for the query that presented itself as she heard Marco's sigh of frustration behind her and his soft footfall toward the door.

By the end of the week, Kelly was certain she was pregnant. Because she didn't want to believe it, she couldn't even imagine the possibility. Until she remembered that first time they made love, unprotected—and the whisper of what she had hoped had been a period afterwards, which obviously hadn't been. And if she had been thinking straight in the weeks that had followed, she would have acknowledged the possibility that she was expecting Marco's child.

But now, with another missed period and a daily condition that had transformed the lining of her stomach into a permanent roller-coaster, the indications were clear. But stubbornly she put the thought aside, hoping against hope that her period would arrive.

On Saturday Marco arrived at nine to collect her and she heard Frederico's excited voice as he rang the doorbell.

But when she opened the door, his little face fell as he saw her pale, gaunt features and shadowed eyes. She knew she looked dreadful despite the bear hug she gave him as he ran into her arms.

'You are still unwell?' Marco asked as she straightened and curved another bright smile on what felt like wooden lips.

'No, I'll be fine.' She shrugged, unable to meet his eyes.

'I'm concerned,' Marco said anxiously. 'Perhaps we should postpone our trip.'

Frederico looked up at her with such disappointment that she waved a dismissive hand and insisted they go. An hour later they were on board the *Sophia* and Kelly was doing her best to fight waves of sickness as Marco turned the boat out to sea.

But by the time they moored at the cove, Kelly admitted defeat.

'Rest,' Marco insisted as she sat on deck looking deathly pale. 'Go down into the cabin and try to sleep,' he instructed, and she went without protest to collapse below for the rest of the morning.

She felt better when she woke and managed to swim with Frederico. She even ate a little afternoon tea from the hamper provided by Isabella.

'I've made reservations at a restaurant in town for the four of us tonight,' Marco told her as they sat under the white canopy on the cushioned chairs. 'Will you feel well enough to join us?'

Kelly said she would and was rewarded with a hug from Frederico. And somehow she made the trip back and promised to be ready for dinner that evening when Marco returned to collect her. It was the last time she would see Frederico and Isabella before they returned to Italy the following week.

It was the last time, too, that she would give in to Marco's insistence that they continue their relationship. In her own way she was beginning damage limitation, attempting to ease the heartache that was an inevitable result of falling in love with a man who could never return the depth and strength of her love.

Kelly was conscious of Marco watching her all evening, as though he knew this was the last time she intended to see him.

Under normal circumstances, she would have enjoyed the intimacy of his gaze, his obvious approval of her sleeveless black gown that fitted every curve of her slender body and long, willowy legs with a discreet elegance. But the gruelling hours on the boat had tested her resources and she prayed that she could end the day—her last few hours with the people she had come to think of as family—with warm appreciation.

But every now and then Marco's beautiful eyes met hers across the lavishly decorated table reserved for them at one of Charbourne's most luxurious hotels. She managed to gaze back into them with a smile, aware that he was keenly assessing her. And that, above all, she had to behave normally in front of Frederico and Isabella.

The waiters danced attendance on them and the food was superb. But Kelly hid her sensitive appetite as she refused the rich dish of the day and ordered a light salad and breast of chicken. Fortunately the evening was so full of talk and laughter that no one noticed.

And when the meal was over and they sat in the elegant lounge that adjoined the hotel's restaurant, she was deeply touched by Frederico's insistence on sitting beside her.

'Papa says you will come to see us in Italy,' he told her as she sipped water instead of the rich, dark coffee that followed their meal.

Kelly flashed a glance at Marco, wondering if he knew how painful it was for her to have to say goodbye to his son. And how difficult he was making the task for her.

'You'll have all your friends to see,' she evaded, returning her soft violet gaze to the young boy's intent stare. 'And your grandmother.'

'And school,' Isabella teased.

'Your English,' Kelly added swiftly, 'will be the best in your class.'

Frederico beamed with delight and fortunately nothing more was said on the subject of her travelling to Italy. When at last it was time for them to leave, Marco caught Kelly by the arm as she was about to climb into the car.

'Thank you for a wonderful, evening,' he whispered as she paused. 'The first of many more, *cara*.'

She smiled sadly, aware of the magical early autumn evening mellowing around them, and for a moment they stared at one another in the crisp night air with the scent of woodsmoke and salt and browning leaves. It was a delicious evening, with a sky full of twinkling stars and a moon of milk. And she carved it into her memory for ever, setting the seal on her decision to tell Marco tomorrow.

It was Monday and everyone had gone, including the reception staff. Only the purr of the cleaning machines could be heard in the background. Marco sat opposite Kelly in the patient's chair, his face carved in stone after the news she had just delivered.

'You are going to Paris on Saturday,' he repeated in a voice filled with disbelief.

She nodded, clenching her hands as she sat in her chair, aware of the silence of her room. She had waited until now to tell him, in a far safer place than the apartment. There he would only have to touch her and she would crumble, forgetting all her resolutions. 'Yes, Saturday.'

'For how long?'

'A fortnight,' she said as she forced herself to stare into the glittering blue eyes. 'I'm overdue seeing Meg and the children. And Jamie is happy to let me go. With your brother returning next week, we'll be sufficiently staffed.'

'Then you will not be here when I leave?'

'No.' She looked away. 'I...I'm afraid not.' When he didn't respond she dragged back her gaze and whispered pleadingly. 'It's best, Marco.'

The look in his eyes devastated her as the last of the evening sunlight slanted in through the blinds, emphasizing the thickness of his lashes as they swept down on his cheeks.

'It was difficult enough last night, saying goodbye to Frederico,' she tried to explain, digging her nails into her palm to keep her focused. 'I can't do it all over again.'

She felt her heart miss a beat as understanding registered on his face and he shook his dark head slowly. 'You are running, Kelly. One day you will have to stop.'

'I have stopped,' she said, her throat full with emotion. 'Here. In Charbourne.'

He paused, his frown digging deeply into his forehead. 'And that is your last word?'

She nodded silently, stiffening her back as he continued to gaze at her. For one terrible moment of weakness she almost gave in. But then she remembered the baby and how, if he knew she was pregnant, he would insist that he stand by her, refuse absolutely to let her go. And she would be too weak to fight, because this decision was costing her every ounce of emotional strength.

There was no way she wanted him to be with her because of their child. Or Sophia. Or for any other reason other than he loved her. She needed to be loved for herself. For the person she was. For all that she comprised. Good and bad. She wanted love that came in one hundred per cent wholeness. And if what he was offering her didn't meet that criterion, she would never settle for less.

'*Cara*, I cannot believe you would make this decision,' he muttered, his body tensing as he regarded her.

She looked up at him under weary eyelids. 'I tried to tell you, tried to explain, Marco. Claiming that I truly believe there was a future for us after you had gone back to Italy would be a lie. You and I know that long-distance relationships rarely work. And I want us to part with good memories and with no recrimination or the chance of what we have, which is so beautiful, going sour.'

And that wasn't even the half of it. Oh, yes, she had gone through all the scenarios in her mind, using them as blocks to her feelings for him. But in the end she had known that all of them could be overcome if he had loved her as much as she loved him.

Then a tide of nausea engulfed her and she knew she must end this conversation. All she wanted to do was crawl into a corner and curl up, but with Marco staring at her like that, and the room swaying, there was every possibility she would fall into his arms and blurt out the whole sorry truth.

She stood up on shaky legs that felt ready to collapse at

any moment, straightening her back and lifting her chin. 'I'm sorry, Marco. Truly.'

For what seemed like an eternity he remained seated, his eyes fixed on her steadily, their stunning brilliance tempered. Then slowly he stood up, easing his body to attention. She thought he was about to reply, but he tightened his mouth and turned and she watched in a haze of misery as his tall body vanished into the hall.

The following day, Marco drove Frederico and Isabella to the airport for their flight home, and in his absence Kelly confirmed her own newly formed plans with Jamie and Meg. Her sister was delighted that she had finally agreed to spend time with them. Even Pierre spoke on the phone to her as did the two children, Natalie, five, and Pierre Junior, four.

She booked her flight from the local airport to Paris and refused to let her mind wander back to Marco. She had no way of knowing how much—or how little—she had upset him with her flat refusal to be deterred from her plans.

But if she showed even the smallest sign of weakening, she knew that her resolution to end their relationship this way would waver. And it had taken all her strength to do what she had done.

On Wednesday, she met Marco in the hall before surgery, his tall form approaching as she walked to her room. She felt as though they had been separated for years and all her instincts were to reach out to him. But as she drew closer, she saw the face of a man she hardly recognized.

'Hello, Marco,' she murmured, taken aback as she looked into his tired, drawn face and eyes that revealed no hint of intimacy. He looked immaculately dressed in an elegant dark suit and white shirt, but his shoulders stiffened the moment he saw her.

'How are you?' he asked so formally that a fist grabbed her heart and she gulped a breath, swallowing back the hurt.

'I'm fine.' She nodded. The silence between them was unnerving. 'Did Frederico and Isabella leave safely?'

He gave her a grim little smile. 'Yes, thank you.'

'I'll miss them,' she acknowledged, and truly meant it, but the normally receptive lines of his face hardened. She said breathlessly, 'About Monday—'

But he held up his hand to stop her, a cold expression in his eyes informing her that whatever she said was irrelevant now. 'It's done with,' he muttered crisply, his soft and melodious accent sounding as though it had been carved from his throat by a chisel. 'I hope your…*holiday* gives you great happiness,' he said with polite efficiency.

She felt as though she had taken a knife and stabbed them both. 'Thank you.'

'Good morning, Kelly.' He offered her the briefest of smiles, moved aside to allow her to pass, then strode to his room.

Kelly felt as if all the life had drained out of her. She managed to stumble to her desk and collapse there, her heart pounding so heavily that, combined with the morning sickness, she felt more wretched than ever.

What have you done, Kelly Anders? a small, lost voice wailed inside her. She knew what she had done. She had ended their affair. On her terms. And that was the way she wanted it. Quick and clean. With as little damage as possible on both sides. Not the way it had been with Dad, when the man she adored had just disappeared like a puff of smoke from her life.

She'd had the chance to say goodbye this time.

And she'd taken it.

CHAPTER THIRTEEN

PARIS in October.

It should have been wonderful. It should have been strengthening and healing. And for all the touring they did, both with the children and Pierre and on their own, exhausting. And perhaps Kelly was exhausted—physically.

They shopped lavishly at the Rue de Faubourg St Honore and conceded a diversion to the Boulevard Haussmann when their budgets went wildly over the top. Pierre took them to his factory in Montmartre and they inspected the incredible reproduction furniture that was handcrafted by his designer-led team of specialist staff.

Natalie and Pierre Junior insisted they visit the Georges Pompedou Centre to mingle among the sixty thousand visitors that watched the mime artists and street entertainers in the piazza each day.

And just when Kelly thought they couldn't fit in any more museums or churches or department stores, they found tiny little markets and cafés in the Latin Quarter and lost themselves for a whole day in the Sorbonne.

Meg insisted they didn't stop, hauling Kelly out after breakfast when the children went to their pre-school until they collected them mid-afternoon. Then they would take them to the gardens or the parks and in the evenings, Pierre would escort them to dinner and perhaps the theatre afterwards.

Kelly was grateful. She had told Meg everything the evening after she had arrived. And Meg, predictably, had offered the sanest of advice.

'We'll fill every moment,' she promised. 'You won't have time to think of him here.'

But Meg had been wrong in that instance. Paris was such a romantic city. And watching young lovers strolling hand in hand brought back memories that Kelly had to deal with, smiling bravely at the world while her heart cramped with pain.

They hadn't even said goodbye.

After that meeting in the hall, Marco had seemed to avoid her. Or had she avoided him? She didn't know. Either way, on the Friday she had left the surgery without seeing him. He had been on call and in desperation she'd waited for the phone to ring that night.

But it had remained silent and that same little voice had whispered, *What do you expect? You've got what you wanted. He's out of your life now. Deal with it.*

'Are you staying with us until Christmas, Aunt Kelly?' Natalie asked before she went to school on Monday. Already she spoke English and French fluently.

'No, but I'll visit you then, darling, if I'm not working,' Kelly said, trying to forget this was the day that Marco flew back to Italy.

'Mummy says you work too hard.'

Kelly hugged her niece. 'Sometimes perhaps.'

'Because you're a doctor.'

'Well, yes. In a way.'

'Will you have any babies like my mummy did?'

Kelly sat back on her heels as the little girl with deep brown eyes and fair hair stared at her curiously. 'I hope so, darling, one day.'

'But you'll have to get married first.'

'Yes, I will.'

Natalie giggled, and Kelly watched her run off to Meg in the kitchen. With breakfast over and the day ahead of them, Kelly and Meg were making their way with the children in the lift from the second-floor apartment to the underground car park.

As Meg drove them out into the sunshine, an aircraft high above glistened in the pale blue sky. Marco would be on his way by now, maybe in that very plane, Kelly reflected as she craned her neck to watch the tiny silver dart high above.

Then, without warning, she felt the tears prick under her long dark lashes, threatening to spill unreasonably down her cheeks. She blinked them back, refusing to allow Natalie's innocent enquiry to expose the wound that she had been trying so hard to conceal.

Marriage was a lifetime away. Her choice, of course, no one else's. But at this moment, sitting with her sister's children in the back of Meg's comfortable car, amidst the heart of a family, the regrets flowed over her.

Marco was gone and now she must pick up the pieces of her life and move on.

It was a cloudy English October morning, with a stiff coastal breeze that bounced seagulls high and low in the Channel air and sea spray that beat a tattoo on the marina walls, when Kelly arrived back in England.

Her fortnight in Paris had revitalized her physically, but the moment she paid the taxi and walked back into her apartment she felt lonelier than she had felt in her life. She'd promised herself to follow Meg's advice and keep busy.

And that's what she did over the weekend, cleaning the rooms that smelt unused and stuffy and letting the air flow through as she dusted, vacuumed and cleaned. Stocking the freezer and shopping for groceries took up several hours and a visit to the marina club, seeing everyone again, filled Sunday evening.

But Monday she dreaded the most. Walking into surgery and talking to the receptionists, then walking past *his* room. She wouldn't look in. She'd just go straight down the hall. Hopefully, her list would be full and she'd be too busy to think of him.

One day at a time, she'd vowed.

And she managed—just. Joking with the receptionists

about her holiday, recounting trivia with light laughter that hid the emptiness inside as she collected her mail in the office, seeing very little as she went on autopilot through her morning's written list.

And then—the walk along the hall, the most terrifying of all. Past Marco's room, now occupied by Antonio. Did she have the courage to walk in and introduce herself? Or would she hurry past and reserve that task for the end of the morning, by which time she would be better prepared to meet her lover's brother?

Correction—her ex-lover's brother.

How many memories would meeting Antonio evoke? she asked herself desperately. How would she be able to stand there and form words if he bore a close resemblance to Marco? A sudden wave of nausea swept over her and she stood still, closing her eyes, to rest her hand on the wall for a moment and compose herself.

Then, groping her way along, she took a breath and walked to the door, which was slightly open. No voices inside. But that incredible scent still lingered. So clear, so musky and yet vibrant. An echo of Marco that sent all her senses into chaos and her stomach churning as she stood poised on the threshold, her fingers shakingly dipped against the wood, her nerve ends tingling with desire and memory and the terrible finality that she herself had set in motion.

Then the door opened without any effort on her part. A tall dark silhouette appeared before her, the height and angle unrecognizable against the morning light from the large south-facing window. She blinked, trying to clear the unpleasant fog that was sealing her eyes and cloying in her throat, but a second or two later her legs gave way at the knees.

'Kelly?'

The deep, unbelievably familiar voice sounded in the distance, like an echo of memory, far away and dreamlike.

She licked her lips, slowly realizing she had blacked out. Fighting the nausea and her apprehension at the same time had simply been too much. And now she was imagining that she heard the one voice in the world that she knew she would never hear again.

'Kelly, sit forward now. I've got you.'

She obeyed the command, unable to do anything else as her stomach heaved and for a moment tiny black spots filled her vision, forcing her to close her eyes as she took a deep breath in. Then, carefully leaning her elbows on her knees, she slowly opened her eyes to focus on a point on the floor. When at last both the floor and room had stopped moving, she eased her vision sideways to the concerned features of the man looking into her face.

Marco's brow was deeply furrowed, his hand lying lightly on her shoulder as she fought the urge to disbelieve the vision that was hunkering down beside her. 'Darling…you fainted…'

She opened her mouth to respond, then gave up, trusting her fingers more than her eyes as she haltingly touched his cheek. 'Marco—you're *here*?'

He nodded, the shadow of a smile on his lips. 'I am here.' He took her hand and clasped it in his own, a deep sigh sliding from his chest. 'Where else would I be?'

'I—You—'

'In Italy? Thousands of miles away from the woman who stole my heart? No. I think not.'

'But…'

He chuckled, the smile finally reaching his eyes. 'Hush, *mi amore*. Regain your breath. Tell me how you are feeling.'

Shocked—devastated—uncomprehending, she wailed silently, but somehow she managed to choke out, 'OK—I think.'

He clicked his tongue disapprovingly. 'Shall we amend that to "as OK as every pregnant woman is in her first trimester"?'

A giant hand inside her chest swung a hammer at her ribs. 'How...how did you know?'

'It was not such a great puzzle,' he said with tender amusement, 'although you took great pains to hide your distress. You were even brave enough to try to eat that wretched piece of chicken at the restaurant after a nightmare of a day on the boat. But I am a doctor, *cara*, and have some insight into your condition—that, together with my instincts, told me that we had made a baby that first night.'

Her pale cheeks flushed as she bit her lip. 'Oh, Marco. I should have told you. But I was so confused. So worried that you would want to stay with me for the baby's sake.'

He stiffened slightly, the breath halting in his throat before he gave another long sigh. 'I do not pretend to understand your reasoning, Kelly. Indeed, the baby means a great deal to me, but you mean more. So much more. Yet I seemed to have failed in all my efforts to convince you of that. Did you really think I would leave England in your absence?' His eyes burned like blue diamonds as they regarded her. 'I am a stubborn man, *cara*—you were warned of that. And you did not heed the warning.'

Kelly remembered Isabella's words that day on the boat. And though she hadn't read any other meaning into them at the time, she now realized how well Isabella knew her uncle. 'I...I couldn't think of another way,' she protested weakly as a guilty flush crept into her pale cheeks.

He lifted his hand and drew a finger along her brow, tenderly curving back her fringe. 'Kelly, it's true I am a stubborn man, but I am also a patient one. And it is a virtue which, as you now see, compensates a little for all the vices.'

Suddenly tears were crowding her eyes and she couldn't see again. Her arms slid over the broad and muscular shoulders hidden under a fine dark blue jacket. 'Marco, I just don't know what to say.'

'Tell me you love me, Kelly, as much as I love you.'

She froze, lifting her head to gaze at him. 'What?'

'I love you, *mi amore*, and I want to spend my life with you. Don't you understand that by now?'

Suddenly she saw that he was looking at her through the eyes of a man in love. She had waited to see that expression and hear those words. And now they were hers, uttered by the man she loved more than life itself.

'I did not realize that I had to earn your trust,' he told her softly. 'But I understand now. Just give me the chance and I will not fail you. I have searched all my life for the love of my life. And now I've found her.'

'But the love of your life was…was *Sophia*,' she faltered, unable to believe she'd made the admission out loud.

'Sophia?' His face darkened in confusion. 'What has Sophia to do with us?'

Kelly looked away, ashamed. 'I saw her photograph, Marco. And…and I saw myself in her so strongly that I…I believed you were trying to replace her—'

'*Dio*, Kelly!' he interrupted loudly, making her jump. 'You thought such a thing? Why did you not tell me?'

'How could I?' she spluttered. 'You would probably have denied it.'

'*Si*, most certainly. For you are nothing like Sophia!'

'But there is such a strong resemblance—'

'Physically,' he cut in, his voice threaded with disbelief. 'In some way. She was beautiful, yes—as you are beautiful. And she was dark-haired and perhaps of a similar height. But that is as far as the likeness goes. You are—how do you say? Chalk and cheese. Opposites.'

She felt her mouth tremble. 'I want to believe you, Marco, but—'

'You must, *cara*! I have told you before, Sophia and I were friends as children,' he sought to explain as his grip tightened over her hands. 'Our families encouraged the marriage and we did not oppose them. No doubt we would have grown contentedly old had not Sophia fallen victim to her illness. But there was nothing of the passion and desire that you inspire in me, Kelly. I have never tasted this before. I want more—I want to know everything there is so to know about the woman who completes me so perfectly.'

She gulped back the tears as his mouth sought hers and he kissed her with soft reassurance until the heat that generated between them burnt their lips like fire. She felt the tears slide slowly down her cheeks and he lifted his hands to rub their damp path with his thumbs.

'How...how can you be so certain of me, Marco?' she whispered as his lips melted against her mouth. 'How do you *know*?'

He looked into her eyes, lifting his hand to slide into her hair, stroking the heavy, silky strands behind her ear. 'Because my heart decrees it,' he said with quiet emphasis.

'And you trust your heart?'

He smiled, lifting her hand to curl it into his own. 'I am Italian, my darling. You should know by now that question is irrelevant.' He lifted her chin and gazed into her eyes. 'No doubt we shall disagree and fight as intensely as we make love,' he whispered, his eyes a deep and brilliant blue. 'And that is what inspires me, fulfils me, endears me to you. I know you will always have something to say, to contribute and, yes, to challenge. But if we believe in our love, we can do anything! The future matters only in as much as we have each other to share it.'

Kelly was smiling through her tears. 'Do you truly believe that?'

'Do you love me, Kelly?'

'Yes, Marco, I love you.'

'Then be confident of our happiness, little one.' He brought hard her against his chest, enfolding her with tender hands. 'That is all that matters.'

She closed her eyes, inhaling the aroma of his shirt and the musky cologne that rose from his warm body, and she kept her eyes closed, her heart feeling as if it was ready to burst with joy as he lifted her face to his and kissed her again.

CHAPTER FOURTEEN

'*ROMA, mi amore*. Where else would I bring you for our honeymoon but the most romantic city in the world?' Marco's soft enquiry was uttered in the reverent silence of the Piazza San Pietro as they paused to gaze at the enormous nativity scene created for the visiting crowds by the Vatican itself.

Kelly swallowed on the heavy lump in her throat, afraid to break the silence as her husband's arms slid around her waist and she nestled down against him, her chin just rising above the high collar of her slim-fitting coat. Their breath curled in the night air as a chorus of midnight chimes echoed around the heart of the Eternal City.

'Beautiful and blessed,' he whispered, taking her in his arms, as they stood, unaware of the other couples who were taking advantage of the late hour and the unique opportunity to witness the yearly splendour of Yuletide Rome.

She looked up at her tall, handsome husband, aware that the last seven days had been the happiest in her life. Their civil wedding in Venice at the Palazzo Cavalli, a private palace filled with stunning Venetian antiques and frescos, had taken place against the backdrop of the famous Grand Canal and Rialto Bridge. A long, stately line of decorated gondolas had borne the guests from their five-star hotel to the Palazzo Cavalli.

Antonio had spared no expense in making their day a fairy-tale wedding. A formally attired official wearing a wide band in the colours of the Italian flag had welcomed each guest. He had honoured each member of the Dallori family and Meg and Pierre and their children with a courteous bow whilst Frederico and Laura's little girl, Maria, had acted as young escorts to the bride and groom.

Kelly's sapphire blue A-line gown, decorated with spiral thread and bead embroidery, was cut cleverly to hide her new curves. The high bateau neckline moulded her figure to perfection under the exquisite Duchesse satin. The sun had shone as though it had been a summer's day and had sparkled on the water like molten gold.

Marco looked stunning in a full dress suit, the fine dark blue cloth of his jacket bearing a subtle brocade that complemented his oyster-coloured waistcoat and silk cravat. He looked tall and elegant as they ascended the steps of the Palazzo, his love-laden eyes meeting Kelly's as the simple marriage ceremony had lasted thirty breathtaking minutes. A translator had interpreted on behalf of the watching assembly and finally Marco had slipped a band of heavy gold on her slim finger.

From that moment on there were wings on their heels. After departing the sumptuous wedding feast held at the hotel, they flew in a privately hired jet to Campi Flegrei in Pozzuoli to gaze on Vesuvius as the sun set in tiers of scarlet blushes behind the majestic silhouette. At night, they watched enchanted, from their hotel balcony as a delicate mist had enshrouded the *golfo*, Vesuvius's magnificent crater.

The next morning they were chauffeured to see the hot mud of Solfatara and on to the cool, tranquil lakes of Fusaro and Miseno to travel over their mirror-like surfaces in a private launch. Every moment of their journey toward Rome had been filled with breathtaking wonder.

'I can't believe we've really visited so many places in one week,' Kelly sighed as she now rested her head on Marco's shoulder and they turned toward the Piazzo Navona. The star-filled sky was an ocean of glittering jewels, the buzz of the city humming like a giant honeybee around them.

During the day they had shopped at the market, gathering

gifts for the family and indulging in the delicious roasted nuts served piping hot from gaily decorated stalls by volatile, cheeky vendors.

Overlooked by the world famous Bernini sculptures in Piazza Navona, they had searched for plastic Josephs and the good-witch figurines of Befana for Frederico's amusement. At home in Capri with his grandmother, he patiently awaited their return the following week and the gifts they had promised to bring with them.

'You are not too tired, *cara*?' Marco asked in concern as they wound their way through the still busy streets.

'Not at all,' she assured him excitedly. 'I could walk all night. I want to see everything. Pompeii, the temples at Paestum, the catacombs...'

He laughed. 'And I will show them to you. But not all in one day. You must rest a little, for your tiny passenger's sake.'

As they walked, Kelly gazed into the brightly lit windows chockfull of souvenirs of the Christ-child and Holy Mother. Christmas had never seemed so poignant as it did now, her own child growing inside her, its tiny form hidden discreetly beneath the soft silk of her dress.

'You will never forget our honeymoon, *cara*,' Marco promised her, his hand clasped firmly around her waist. 'Rome is the most intoxicating city in the world. And I want my bride to be intoxicated for ever—with her husband.' He grinned, stopping as they came to a secluded little oasis of calm near the Piazza di Spagna. Mischievously he slid his hand under the fold of her coat to the gentle swell of her stomach. 'Here, in Rome, our little one's life will be blessed, just as our marriage is blessed.'

Kelly never would have thought it possible that her honeymoon would be spent in the heart of this ancient and romantic city, with Marco's arms tightly around her as they gazed up at the column dedicated to the Blessed Virgin. Here, just a few days before, the Pontiff himself had placed flowers in honour of one very special mother's conception. And now, in the holy silence of Christmas, Kelly silently whispered a prayer for her husband and darling child.

I love you both. Dearly...

Her eyes filled with tears as Marco cupped her chin between tender fingers and stared into her eyes. 'I promise that we shall have a long and happy life, *cara*.' His voice was suddenly serious, his broad shoulders lifting under his dark, elegant jacket. 'Do you believe me, Kelly?'

'I believe you, darling.'

'No more doubts?'

'None,' she acknowledged truthfully. 'As long as I have you, that's all that matters.'

'Oh, *cara*, I am such a lucky man,' he breathed as he brought his mouth down to cover her parted lips.

No, she was the lucky one, she reminded herself fiercely as his lips burnt over hers and sought her hungry response. From the moment she had met Signora Dallori at Canzone with Antonio and Laura after their return to England, she had begun to realize her life had changed for ever.

They had welcomed her without reservation. Signora Dallori had embraced her with deep and genuine affection and Laura, sensing her vulnerability, had become a special friend in the weeks that followed.

And when Kelly, at the request of Signora Dallori, had returned to Capri to stay for a short holiday at the beautiful clifftop villa, all her doubts had been washed away. On that wonderful island of dreams, her love for Marco had grown to unfathomable proportions.

'Frederico will be a wonderful son,' Mamma Dallori had assured her one day when they had been alone together. 'And Marco a loving husband. He is, as his father was, an honourable man.'

Kelly had tried to hide her tears of joy and gratitude at the reassurance the older woman had provided. She would never forget that holiday, coming to know Frederico and the Dallori family as though they were her own people.

She had been stunned by Capri's beauty—the famous Blue Grotto and its underground passages over which little rowboats glided in the extraordinary translucent water, the carob- and olive-tree-covered peninsula of the Sorrentine, the natural arches of the graceful Faraglioni. She had never seen such breathtaking beauty in her life before. And by the time she had returned to England, her heart had been entirely won by Marco's enchanting island.

Not that they had decided where to live—yet. That was a decision they would reach together after their honeymoon, and Kelly found herself now willing to trust in the future. She was the happiest woman in the world. There were no obstacles she couldn't overcome, as long as she had Marco's love and support.

'You're shivering,' Marco muttered anxiously. 'Shall we go back to the hotel?'

'No. I'm excited, not cold.' She raised her gloved hands to lay them lightly on his shoulders. He was such a handsome man. But his features had seemed to have changed over the last few months, his heavy-lidded eyes becoming even more seductive as they had relaxed and come to know one another better.

His high cheek-bones still looked sculptured from stone, reminding her of the wonderful Bernini sculptures in the Piazza Navona. His mouth was still full and sensual and his kisses were still the most passionate she had ever tasted.

But there was something different…

It was as though love had transformed him, warming the cold and lonely void that Sophia's absence had stamped on him. But now she no longer feared his dead wife's memory. Now that she was secure in his love and in Frederico's, Sophia's memory had been put to rest. And as she gazed up into his face, she knew that, whatever life had in store for them, she was no longer afraid.

This man would never disappear in a puff of smoke. He would always come home to her. He would remain beside her in all seasons, come what may.

'I shall have to wait just a little longer to hold my bride,' he said crooking a smile that tested all her self-control.

After a moment's thought, her violet eyes shone up at him with a flirtatious gleam. '*Questo dipende, mi amore,*' she replied in her attractively accented Italian. 'Maybe I *am* a little cold!'

He laughed aloud, hugging her to him. 'Then I know of the perfect way to warm you, my lovely wife.'

And pausing briefly to glimpse at the stars sparkling above them, they changed direction, retracing their steps through the Eternal City toward the hotel.

Kelly gazed up at the fresco-covered ceiling, her eyes tracing the intricate gold and blue patterning that framed the cherubs and voluptuous goddesses adorning the ceiling of the hotel's honeymoon suite.

Little arrows spun from the bows of the winged archers, piercing the heart of the central figure; a beautiful female form reclined on the smooth grass by a lake, the beasts of the forest crouched around her. Beside her, a youth rested, his naked and perfectly formed body at ease, his gaze fixed on her voluptuous body, his hand lying proprietorially on her hip. An arrow had pierced his heart, too, the glint of gold on his breast shining mystically under the special lighting that had been contrived for the painting.

Over the three nights that she had lain in the bed, she had come to know the story intimately, delighting in its message each time she had fixed her eyes on the heavenly saga above. And as Marco had joined her each night, his bronzed and naked body unchallenged by the youth's beauty above, they had paused to gaze up at the fresco.

And each night Marco had taken her in his arms and made love to her beneath the romantic scene, the huge honeymoon bed bearing their weight with ease, as did the forest floor of the lovers above.

His fingers had loosened her gown, drawing the single silk straps over her shoulder and down the smooth slope of her arms. The movement had been so patient and tender that she had almost been ready to scream at him to make love to her. But his eyes had warned her that he had not been ready to set her alight so swiftly and his caresses had born her to the height of joy and pleasure which had flooded into every part of her body, from the tip of her head down to her toes.

And now, with two nights to go until Christmas Day, the sound of the city drifted in through the open balcony windows, like a musical accompaniment to their night of love. To choose a Christmas wedding and honeymoon had surpassed all her dreams. And knowing that Frederico was safely in the bosom of the family and waiting to accompany them on a special post-Christmas holiday, skiing in the Alps, had banished any doubts they might have had at leaving him at such a time.

'I want the most potent magic in the world for our wedding,' Marco had told her as they had made plans that autumn.

Even when Marco had returned to Capri for a few short weeks without her, missing him had only served to deepen her convictions about their future together, be it in England or Italy. And when Antonio had happily released her from her contract and suggested that she join Marco well in advance of their wedding, she had gratefully accepted his suggestion.

And now, as she lay in Marco's arms, her body shuddering with the delight of fulfilment and radiant with the new life that they had conceived, Kelly gazed up into the enigmatic features of the woman in the fresco. Confident in the knowledge that she had found her soul mate, her eyes revealed the truth of the forest mystery.

She was not lying on a bed of silk sheets as Kelly was, but in nature's own garden, just as the two first lovers had rested at the beginning of creation. Yet her expression was of divine bliss, and Kelly knew that her own features re-

flected that joy. What more perfect setting for either o
them than in the centre of Rome's eternally beating heart'

'I love you, *mi amore*,' Marco whispered as his eye:
darkened, then blazed once more. 'And I will love you fo
ever. In this world and the next.'

A pact Kelly knew they would keep, as all true lover:
were destined to keep, throughout the passage of time.

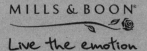

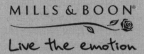

4 Books
and a surprise gift!

We would like to take this opportunity to thank you for reading this Mills & Boon® book by offering you the chance to take FOUR more specially selected titles from the Medical Romance™ series absolutely FREE! We're also making this offer to introduce you to the benefits of the Reader Service™—

- ★ FREE home delivery
- ★ FREE gifts and competitions
- ★ FREE monthly Newsletter
- ★ Books available before they're in the shops
- ★ Exclusive Reader Service discount

Accepting these FREE books and gift places you under no obligation to buy; you may cancel at any time, even after receiving your free shipment. Simply complete your details below and return the entire page to the address below. *You don't even need a stamp!*

YES! Please send me 4 free Medical Romance books and a surprise gift. I understand that unless you hear from me, I will receive 6 superb new titles every month for just £2.60 each, postage and packing free. I am under no obligation to purchase any books and may cancel my subscription at any time. The free books and gift will be mine to keep in any case.

M3ZEF

Ms/Mrs/Miss/Mr ....Initials..
BLOCK CAPITALS PLEASE

Surname ....

Address...

....

....Postcode ....

Send this whole page to:
UK: The Reader Service, FREEPOST CN81, Croydon, CR9 3WZ
EIRE: The Reader Service, PO Box 4546, Kilcock, County Kildare (stamp required)

Offer not valid to current Reader Service subscribers to this series. We reserve the right to refuse an application and applicants must be aged 18 years or over. Only one application per household. Terms and prices subject to change without notice. Offer expires 28th November 2003. As a result of this application, you may receive offers from Harlequin Mills & Boon and other carefully selected companies. If you would prefer not to share in this opportunity please write to The Data Manager at the address above.

Mills & Boon® is a registered trademark owned by Harlequin Mills & Boon Limited.
Medical Romance™ is being used as a trademark.